Island Magic

BY

MICHELLE GARREN FLYE

Published by Michelle Garren Flye

Copyright October 2014

Author photo by Jenn Reno Photography

For Phyllis and Wayne.

Thank you for introducing me to Mexico.

Acknowledgments:

I am doomed to never leave myself enough space for these acknowledgements. I squeeze in long lists of the people I love, but trust me when I say, these people are far from afterthoughts. Without them, I might not even bother!

Rebekah, thank you for reading this manuscript in its infant stages and offering words of reassurance and wisdom. Lisa, Jennifer, Katie, Sherri, AM, Suzanne, Mary Kathryn, Candice, Rebecca, Andrea, Melissa, Jeff, Ginger, Celia, Todd and Georgiana (in no particular order!), thank you so much for your continued support and help in getting the word out about my books. Thank you, Most Flye Street Team!

A special recognition to the ladies of the Trent Woods book club who not only read *Close Up Magic*, but invited me to their meeting to discuss it. That was, without doubt, one of the highlights of my writing career thus far.

And finally, to the most important people in my life. My wonderful husband Chris, who is the inspiration and sounding board and support system for all my books. My children, Josh, Ben and Jessi: thanks for putting up with my tapping fingers on the keyboard! And to my extended family, Mama, Daddy, Bruce, Bobby, Brandon, Phyllis and Wayne who all do their part to encourage and support me in my efforts.

Thank you all!

Prologue

Night fell slowly in the Caribbean, and when it came, it was complete. Especially in the little bar on the beach that Logan loved. Even the tiki torches on the boardwalk only spread small radii of flickering glow around their poles. The rest was a dark, secret haven.

From his lighted oasis beneath the thatch-roofed bar, he watched the patrons of the resort milling around, coming in from the dark beach, usually hand-in-hand with someone else. Occasionally a group of young men would collide with a group of young women and soon they would pair off and head into dark corners. All Logan had to do was make their drinks and chat. No interference required on his part. He was like a voyeuristic benefactor, watching them leave with nothing but good feelings.

When he first spotted Rachel in the bar, then lost sight of her in a crowd of college kids, he thought he must be mistaken. He frowned, craning his neck. It certainly had looked like Rachel. Nora's best friend, the maid of honor at his wedding to a woman who was now dead. But what would

Rachel be doing there? He hadn't seen her in years, but he didn't believe in coincidence. Magic, but not coincidence.

He recognized the long, luxurious hair and the lovely features, even though they had a hard edge he didn't recall. And what was up with the slinky dress? Rachel had always seemed so strait-laced he'd figured she would be a suburban soccer mom by now. This was no soccer mom. This wasn't even the beautiful, gentle woman Nora had known in the years after their marriage.

She sat at a table not far from the bar. She was alone, but everything about her said she had no intention of remaining that way. Logan noticed several men glancing her way. He couldn't blame them. Her raven hair fell over one bare shoulder, her sleeveless red sundress setting off her tan. He couldn't take his eyes off her, and he shouldn't be looking at Rachel that way. Not Nora's best friend.

When the waitress took her order for a frozen margarita with salt, Logan intercepted it from Ramon. "Sorry, man." He grinned at his friend and fellow bartender. "I'm gonna deliver this one personally."

Ramon gave him a mock growl. "Earn me a good tip if you're gonna pull rank on me, amigo."

Logan flashed him a smile and vaulted the bar neatly, landing on the other side to appreciative looks from a group of young women. He saluted them, picked up the margarita and crossed to the table. "Your margarita, señorita."

She raised beautiful dark eyes to meet his. The raw sensuality in that gaze left him breathless. She smiled, playing along as if she had no idea who he was. "Muchas gracias, señor. To what do I owe the special delivery?"

He glanced left and right, then sat across from her, leaning over the table as if to keep their conversation covert. "Between you and me, I've been told I'm overly concerned with our guests' satisfaction."

The curve of her lips deepened and he knew she'd sensed a double entendre in his words. He wanted to laugh but didn't give in to the impulse. He wasn't even certain he'd meant to flirt with her, but it had come out that way. He'd spent so many years on stage, his career so dependent on reading his audience, yet he couldn't seem to see through Rachel's carefully guarded exterior. She was so unlike the woman he remembered, it worried him. Enough so he stepped over a boundary he hadn't crossed in years.

He beckoned her closer. When she obliged, her expression highly amused, he said quietly, "Do you believe in magic?"

****

8

The light touch of his breath on her ear sent a pleasant tingle of electricity through Rachel's body. Maybe it was the way he pretended not to know her instead of demanding instantly what she was doing there and why she looked the way she did. He'd have every right, of course. She probably shouldn't have just shown up this way. Why the hell did I? There are thousands of resorts in Cancun, but here I am on his island, a hundred miles away from those resorts and reachable only by plane. I might as well be on Fantasy Island.

The idea of this exceptionally tall, dark-skinned, very handsome man as a modern-day Mr. Roark was close enough to the truth of what Rachel knew she'd come searching for so she shied away from it. Magic wouldn't help her now. Even if she did believe in it.

But maybe it had been what had brought her here to Isla Foriscura with her life in shambles around her. She'd told herself she wanted nothing but fun and a chance to spend her alimony, but in her broken heart, she knew the truth lay in the question the widower husband of her dead best friend had just asked her.

Do you believe in magic?

To the best of her knowledge he hadn't performed magic since Nora died. Since he'd retired to his private island turned reclusive resort in the Caribbean. But she had no intention of asking him about it because that would break the little spell of pretense between them.

Instead she sipped the margarita, enjoying the tangy drink mixed with the salt from the rim. She let her lips part a little just before answering, noticed the way he focused on her mouth. "Should I?"

"Maybe." He snagged an empty glass from a passing waitress and set it on the table in front of her.

She frowned. "Am I supposed to do something with that?" She glanced around, noticing that a little crowd of interested onlookers had gathered, including the waitresses. Did they know something she didn't?

He shook his head, taking her hand and pulling her to her feet. "Not that." He twirled her around so she stood with her back to his chest, one of his hands on her waist. She wasn't a short woman and she was wearing heels, but Logan was exceptionally tall. Over six feet tall and well built, he dwarfed her, but he adjusted his stance so his head was just over her shoulder.

She could feel the heat of his breath on her neck and she closed her eyes. If he weren't Ian Logan—if she really didn't know him—she would have enjoyed this. She would have let her body mold against his, felt his response, reveled in the feel of his firm body…

She forced herself to open her eyes, maintain her distance. Dear God, how had she forgotten what a sexy man he was? Ian Logan had everything. Money, talent, looks, confidence…and a broken heart the last time she saw him. Still, she wondered what it would be like spending the night in his arms. Would it be different from all the other nights? She remembered Kevin and her heart shuddered. Her voice came out sounding slightly more acidic than she'd intended. "What, then?"

Unperturbed by her change of tone, he raised his free arm and pointed at the stars. "Those."

She frowned. "I beg your pardon?"

"Pick one."

"Just one?" His gentle mysterious tone intrigued her, but she couldn't help mocking him a little bit.

He laughed. "Just one. I can only catch one at a time."

"Oh, you can catch one, can you?" She snorted, scanned the skies and decided to play along. Obviously she'd been wrong about him not practicing magic. He had a little bar trick he used to amuse the crowd and probably to pick up women. Well, it wouldn't work well on her unless she wanted it to. She chose a bright star low on the horizon. "That one."

"Perfect." He moved away, leaving her bare back surprisingly cool in the evening breeze. He handed her the glass. "Hold that." He gazed into the distance for a moment, then reached out as if plucking something from the air in front of him. It reminded her of the days when she used to catch fireflies as a child and she fended off the jolt of nostalgia with difficulty.

He turned back, his hand closed and a mischievous expression playing on his features. She'd forgotten the other people clustered around them. She'd almost forgotten that she knew Logan and he knew her. They were two strangers in a bar and she wanted to believe the expression in his warm brown eyes was just for her. That he wasn't still a showman and that all of this was for her benefit alone.

He raised one eyebrow, holding his hand close to his face. "You didn't answer my question earlier. Do you believe in magic?"

She thought of everything that had brought her to this point, everything that had gone wrong in her life and what she'd lost. How could she believe in magic now? Without pausing to doctor her answer, she replied honestly. "No. Not anymore."

His smile faded, but not as if he'd lost confidence. More as if he felt her pain. She looked away, uncomfortable, wishing he hadn't spotted her. Or maybe that she hadn't come. He didn't falter, however. Instead he placed his closed hand over the glass and took her free hand, placing it on top of his. In a swift, practiced movement, he opened his hand and pulled it away, pushing hers down on top of the glass. "Do you believe now?"

She gasped, looking at the blue-white light hovering in the glass. What could it be but the star she'd requested? She turned the glass in her hands as the little crowd applauded and he bowed. No matter which way she turned the glass, the light shimmered back at her. She stared in amazement, barely feeling it when he led her back to the table and helped her put the glass down without taking her hand away.

She tore her eyes away from the glimmering light, trying to focus on him. "This is a trick, right?"

"The best magic always leaves you wondering." He smiled a little, but she could see the shadow of sorrow still hovering in his eyes.

"What happens if I move my hand?" She glanced back at the glass.

"The light goes out." He shrugged. "You can't keep a star captive forever."

"No. You can't." His words filled her with sadness and she knew why she'd come there. To his island. To him. Because of all people, Ian Logan knew that nothing lasted forever. Love, life, stars. She gave the light in the jar a final look of regret before taking her hand away from the top. It flickered and died. She raised her eyes to Logan's. "It's a neat trick, Logan. And thanks, but I stopped believing in magic a long time ago."

Summoning a flirtatious smile and a little wiggle into her hips, she moved out of the circle of light around the bar, feeling the darkness descend in a wave of welcome obscurity. She knew another bar down the beach where the young men were sexy and ready to get laid and didn't bother making her feel like she mattered to do it.

Chapter 1

Three floors down from Rachel's window handsome, tanned men dressed in white moved around the pool, setting up chairs, sweeping away small bits of trash, piling clean white towels on bamboo stands. Rachel watched their smooth movements with all the admiration she would feel for a ballet. They were coordinated, efficient, pleasant to observe.

They reminded her a little of the cast members she'd seen at Disney World when she was last there. The memory brought a jab of pain sharp enough to penetrate the morning fog. She'd been so full of hope then. So sure it wouldn't be the last time she believed in magic.

The bedsheets rustled and a tousled dark head emerged. The handsome college kid grinned at her, teeth white against his olive skin. Where was he from again? Spain? She struggled to remember at least that much. His name was out of the question. She never remembered names. How old was he, anyway? She hoped at least twenty-one. She didn't want to think she'd spent a passionate night in the arms of anyone technically young enough to be her son. He's still too young for a thirtysomething divorcee. Her years weighed on her for a second before she shook them off impatiently.

He held out a hand. "Come back to bed."

The invitation was eloquently stated and absurdly inviting to have been uttered by someone so young. However old he was, he certainly had experience in the area of making love. And he had the face and body of a fallen angel. Curly, jet-black hair, brown eyes, lush lips. His bare skin smooth and his muscles rock hard... She shook herself out of the memory, making her voice cold on purpose. "You need to go."

He laughed and rolled over onto his back, stretching. "You don't mean that, mi reina."

My Queen. Spanish. She'd at least remembered that right. Rachel felt ludicrously relieved, which firmed up her determination. She needed to get this kid, ah hell, this boy out of her room before she fell back into bed with him. Drunk sex was one thing—the only thing she could afford. Making love sober the morning after was another. She turned away. "It's late. I have things to do."

He was silent. She'd hurt him. She closed her eyes. It was better this way. If he fell into the dark hole of her heart, he'd never survive it. She turned, finding his clothes in a pile on the floor. She picked them up and tossed them to him. "Here you go. You've got a room here, right? Go take a shower." She let herself smile gently at him. "Look, I don't mean to hurt you. Last night was...mmm." She laughed a little. "You're very good. But you're barely old enough for me. Take my advice and stick with girls for now. Give yourself another ten years before you try with a woman my age. At least by then you'll be interesting."

He said nothing, but she could see both hurt and anger in his eyes. He was a boy, after all. She sighed, turning her back, hearing him dressing. Loneliness pulsed in her chest. She felt him pause behind her, close enough so she could feel the heat of his body. Deciding it would do no one any good to send him away damaged, she turned, her lips curved in a hard, sexy smile. "Gracias, mi bello. I enjoyed your company last night. Very much."

The boy still looked adorably rumpled, his shirt unbuttoned to reveal the fine chest she'd found so irresistible. He held his shoes in one hand, and he opened his mouth to say something. She stopped him with a finger to her lips, then kissed him gently and patted his cheek. "Go find yourself someone nice, sweetheart."

As the door closed behind him, her cell phone rang. She glanced at it, considered not answering. Then she picked it up and pushed the button without bothering to look at the caller ID. It was one of two people calling...the only two people who still cared enough to call. And she knew it was more guilt than love that drove them to keep tabs on her.

"Hello."

"Rachel? God. Thank God. Are you okay?" Angela's voice trembled over the airwaves between Mexico and North Carolina.

"Sure. I'm fine. Why wouldn't I be?" Pleased by her nonchalant tone, Rachel strolled casually to the minibar, opening it. Deciding it was too early to drink, especially the overpriced little bottles in the minibar, she shut the door carefully. The poolside bar would open at eleven. She thought of Logan and smiled a little. Would he be bartending again? Did a multi-billlionaire ex-magician tend his own bar often? Of course, Logan could do whatever he damn well pleased, probably. Just as she could.

And Logan might be off limits due to their history, but from the looks of his employees and guests, she'd have plenty of options to take his place. The Spanish kid had been great, but she hungered for something a little...more. Someone more her equal with a prayer of surviving the sucking void in her heart that no amount of fruity alcohol could fill.

"Rachel! God, are you even listening?" Her sister's voice cut through Rachel's musings.

"Not really." Rachel searched for her room key and found it next to her purse. She didn't need the purse, so she tossed it in the room safe with her iPad. As long as she didn't leave the resort—and the island was the resort—she could charge anything she wanted to her room key. And why would she leave the island? It had everything she wanted. Six bars, a three-acre pool, access to the beach, several five-star restaurants and some nice boutique stores. Everything she needed to spend her alimony in style.

"Please come home, Rachel. Or at least tell me where you are. We need you. Kevin is really worried—"

"Don't you dare mention his name to me." Rachel kept her voice dead although she felt bile surge into her throat. "Not you, of all people."

Her sister fell silent. Rachel picked up the room key, which was attached to a plastic bracelet. She slid it over her wrist and swallowed the bitterness in her mouth. "Besides, I'm fine."

"Where are you?" Angela's voice echoed with concern. Or guilt.

Rachel walked over to the window and looked down at the pool again. Most of the workers had finished their dance and left, but one remained. She gave a start of surprise. Logan.

Damn, he was everywhere. Her heart beat faster as she watched him.

He perched on one of the empty deck chairs, alone. He held a smoking white cylinder in one hand, but he didn't raise it to his lips. Rachel noticed his white shirt was unbuttoned, revealing excellent pectorals and a washboard stomach. What would it be like to touch that stomach?

"Please tell me where you are," Angela pleaded again, interrupting Rachel's musings.

"Heaven," she breathed, smiling for a moment at the lustful thoughts in her head. As she watched, Logan tossed the unsmoked cigarette on the ground and stepped on it as he stood. He didn't bother picking it up. He turned and she caught a glimpse of his eyes, dark and smoldering, and she sighed. "Or hell."

She hung up.

****

Logan held the burning cigarette between his thumb and forefinger, even though he wasn't a smoker. He could go days without smoking and never even think about it. Smoking, like most everything else in his life, was an affectation.

Except this place. This is real. Isla Foriscura, his little haven in the middle of the Caribbean, was the only thing real about him anymore. The rest was illusion. The lustful looks of the women, the nights he spent drinking a little too much trying to forget, the mornings when he could very easily have stayed in bed. None of that was real.

She was real. Rachel. She was really here, but it wasn't really her. He frowned at the cigarette, aware that the others had finished the job he'd started with them, but not ready to move yet. He turned the problem of Rachel over and over in his mind. I stopped believing in magic a long time ago.

That wasn't the Rachel he remembered, not that he knew her except for Nora's description: beautiful, carefree, loving and loveable. She'd sent him an invitation to her wedding a few years ago, but he hadn't gone. He'd sent her a lovely crystal vase instead with a card wishing her well. Who was the guy? Keith? Ken? It didn't matter. Obviously he was out of the picture and he'd taken most of the woman Nora had loved with him.

What happened to you, Rachel?

And then there was this day. His birthday. Nora always made a big deal out of birthdays. Probably why Logan hadn't celebrated his since her death. He looked down at the cigarette in his fingers and wound it through them, watching it with interest as it moved, seemingly of its own accord, although he knew it was little flexes of the muscles he'd developed over his years performing sleight of hand magic tricks.

Tricks. The word gave him a sour taste in his mouth. It was all tricks. He tossed the cigarette on the tiles and stepped on it as he stood. He could sit there all day brooding or he could get up and live. He'd always known those were his choices, and he'd chosen life a long time before.

Besides, he had a lot to live for. After retiring from the public world at the height of his success and the lowest point of his life, he'd discovered this place. His retreat. He bought the little oasis on the edge of the calm blue Caribbean and built a retreat for people like him, who, tired of the world, could leave it for a while.

Of course, not everyone who came was broken. Logan had seen his fair share of those like him who needed to heal and he'd seen those who just wanted to escape, but for the most part his visitors were well-to-do and just looking to have a good time. Some were even content with their lot in life. And it didn't hurt that many of the women were very beautiful and usually quite willing to indulge in a brief vacation romance with an ex-magician turned hotel entrepreneur.

It wasn't just the hotel anymore, either. Logan's paradise now encompassed a spa, three five-star restaurants, several fine boutiques, a golf course and a swimming pool that could probably be considered a water park. Everything you could need to have the fabulous vacation of your dreams, all in one resort. In the five years he'd been there, Logan had made more money than he imagined his career as a grand illusionist in New York, Las Vegas and Hollywood would have netted him in twice the time.

Maybe it's because magic possessions tend to disappear. He couldn't help a painful little smile at the thought. It was true, after all. He'd owned a lovely home and even had a wife and daughter during those days, but because he was never home, his wife was gone and his happy home had vanished. He was lucky to get to see his daughter a couple of times a year now.

Logan shook off the negative thoughts and stretched, preparing for the day and making his usual resolution. Today wouldn't slip by without leaving a distinguishing mark on his soul. Today would be special.

"You missed a spot."

He paused in the midst of his stretch and dropped his arms to his sides, turning at the familiar voice. Rachel stood there, long, blue-black hair and dark glasses against smooth tanned skin. Yes. She could leave a mark. He could see her better in the bright sunlight, but he still couldn't read her. She looked like a Hollywood starlet, not like the girl next door who'd been best friends with his wife. "Pardon?"

She lowered the glasses a little on her nose, her dark eyes sweeping his body with frank admiration. He raised his eyebrows a little in surprise at the lusty gaze. Not that a woman's appreciation of his body was an anomaly, but he'd never experienced it so openly before. He found it both arousing and a little unsettling receiving it from this particular source.

Her lips curved into something that wasn't quite a smile, as if she knew what he was thinking. She raised her eyes to meet his briefly and shoved the glasses back up her nose. Then she waved a hand at the unsmoked cigarette that still smoldered on the pool deck. "Over there."

Bemused, he glanced in the indicated direction, pretending not to understand. "I don't see anything."

She considered him for a moment, her arms folded over her chest. Then she shrugged as if it didn't really matter. "Whatever. Just didn't want you to get any complaints."

"Right." He grinned. "Well, if it will make you feel better." He bent, palmed the cigarette and showed her his empty hands. "See? All gone."

"Very good." She pretended to applaud. "Between that trick last night and this one, you've got a whole routine going, Logan. Do you do birthday parties now?"

"Only for very special people."

Silence stretched between them for a moment. She broke it first, a smile a lot more like what he remembered touching her lips. "It's good to see you again."

"I'd like to say the same thing." He reached for her hand, giving it a friendly squeeze, but still uncertain about her transformation.

She put her hand on top of his, drawing attention to both the perfectly manicured red fingernails and the diamond tennis bracelet adorning her wrist. Logan touched the bracelet with a finger. She glanced down and shrugged. "Spoils of war, I guess you'd say."

"Oh?" He raised his eyebrows.

"Got it in the divorce." She laughed out loud, pulling her hands away. "Actually, I got pretty much everything in the divorce. Except my sister. The cheating bastard got her, but he's welcome to her."

He frowned. "I'm sorry. I hadn't heard. I've been pretty out of the loop."

She waved his comment away, tossing her head. "Ancient history. But that's why I'm here. You always talked about this island as a healing place. Well, I'm here to be healed. And spend my alimony."

"I see." He stepped behind the towel counter, surreptitiously dropping the cigarette butt he'd palmed in the trashcan. He started piling towels on the countertop. Neat stacks of five. Enough to supply the need for the first rush of patrons, but not enough to be overwhelming or encourage waste. He'd perfected the system and passed it along to countless other pool boys over the years, but it was sometimes soothing to participate in the process himself.

Her presence wasn't exactly soothing, however. Or maybe it was his reaction to her presence. He glanced up at her. "Can I offer you a towel? Of course, technically the pool doesn't open for another forty-five minutes."

"But you practically run the place." Her tone mocked him in a flirtatious way. She leaned on the counter across from him, giving him an excellent view of her cleavage. He raised an eyebrow, pointedly lifting his gaze to meet hers.

"That is true." He paused in his quest to stack the towels neatly and perfectly on the counter. "I suppose I could give you a VIP pass."

"Ooh. That sounds nice. What, exactly, does it entitle me to?" As she spoke, she discarded the thin boy-friend style pullover she wore, revealing a red string bikini and an absolutely perfect body. Dear God, had she always looked like this? He'd never seen her in less than jeans and t-shirt and he wished like crazy she'd put the goddamn pullover back on, maybe with a pair of shapeless sweatpants to match.

Damn it if she wasn't breaking all the rules. He'd played this game enough to know the truly attractive and intelligent women were the ones you had to work the hardest to get anywhere with. And Rachel was not one he should want to get anywhere with anyway. But if she was going to break the rules, why the hell shouldn't he?

"Hello?" She laughed, leaning even further over the counter and tapping him on the forehead with finger. "You still there, Logan? What does my VIP pass entitle me to? Maybe a little help with the sun block?"

He considered for a moment longer, forcing his heart rate and respiration to slow with all the concentration he'd used during his escape acts. If she could break the rules, he'd just have to re-write them. He snagged her hand before she could retreat. "Is that all you want?"

Her eyes sparkled with interest. "Do you have something else to offer?"

In spite of himself, he'd warmed to her game. He lifted her hand to his lips, kissing the knuckles, then, his eyes on hers, brushing his lips over the sensitive skin of her inner wrist. Her eyes widened a little, her lips parting, and she sounded breathless when she replied. "Oh my. You just might."

He straightened, dropping her hand as if he hadn't just crossed yet another line with her. "Let's have dinner and you catch me up on what I've missed out on. I'll pick you up at seven."

She hesitated, then shrugged. "Why not? I'll try to stay out of trouble until then." She walked away, waving over her shoulder. In spite of himself, he couldn't help admiring her lovely legs, firm buttocks, the dimple at the small of her back and the way her long hair swung past her shoulder blades.

She spread the towel over a chair and sat, stretching long legs in front of her and pointedly not looking at him. Something niggled at the back of his consciousness, and he knew he wouldn't be able to relax until he'd addressed it. She was Rachel, but she wasn't. Rachel didn't move that way, as if she knew every male eye within a mile was focused on her. Rachel was real, not the façade he saw before him.

And Rachel believed in magic.

What happened to her? Divorce couldn't have turned her into this. Nora's death had been hard on her. He'd seen it then, even through his own grief. But she'd survived it. She'd moved on. He'd believed then that eventually she would be happy. She wasn't happy now. Beautiful, independent, obviously at least somewhat wealthy—but he couldn't help but think that she was on a self-destructive track of her own making.

He turned away, determination tightening his jaw. He'd find out what had changed her so much even if what he found was worse than anything he could imagine.

****

Rachel stretched, trying her best to enjoy the warmth of the tropical sun on her skin, but she couldn't stop thinking about Logan. *Jesus, Nora, I'm sorry. I shouldn't be flirting with him like I did, but damn...* She remembered the night before when he'd placed her hand over the glass with the glowing blue-white light in it and her frustration intensified.

A star. How the hell did he do that? She felt uncomfortably hot at the memory of his touch. *Maybe she'd been right to walk away last night after all. What the hell?* When she'd come here, he'd been nothing but the husband of her dead best friend. Even if she had remembered the way he'd spoken of the island as a place of healing. Even if she had thought at the time that maybe he was her salvation. *I still can't want him. Not like that. Not this bad.*

So bad, in fact, she wasn't certain she'd be able to relax in the warm sun for thinking about the feel of his hands on her skin. And the fact that she didn't actually know how his hands would feel only frustrated her more.

She sat up, looking around her. Time lost meaning in the tropics, she'd found, and right now what might have been hours must only have been minutes. No other guests peopled the pool deck. Logan had disappeared, too, although a few white-clothed, very beautiful people who were obviously staffers bustled around the little poolside bar. None of them acknowledged her at all, making her wonder if Logan had warned them off. Not a single quirked eyebrow or smirk was cast her way.

Logan. She flopped back onto her deck chair, thinking of him. It was as if the light touch of his lips on the interior of her wrist had started a heart-deep yearning she hadn't thought she was still capable of...

Do you believe in magic? His lips brushing her ear...

No, but maybe you could help me with that.

She sat up, looking at the bar with irritation. Was it really only ten-thirty in the morning? Another half an hour before the bar opened. She longed for the sweet poison of alcohol in her system. Something to dull the persistent pounding in her veins, the memory of his eyes when he looked at her. The sense that she was betraying the memory of a woman who'd been more than a friend. A woman who'd been almost a sister to her. Better than a sister, as it turned out. She gritted her teeth. Get it...under...control...girl.

"Miss Rachel?" The girl's voice was tentative.

Rachel's head snapped around, her first impulse one of irritation. Until she noted the mimosa on the girl's tray. She frowned, partly in an attempt not to snatch the drink immediately. "Yes." She raised her eyebrows. "Can I help you?"

"Mr. Logan's compliments, ma'am." The young girl executed a surprisingly graceful curtsy as she set the drink on the table beside Rachel.

"Oh." Rachel blinked. "Thank you."

The waitress nodded and turned away. Rachel waited a moment, then reached to her side and picked up the glass. Dear God. It smells so good. She no longer even cared if she had a problem with the alcohol that was her only defense against what had become reality. Well, not her only defense, if she were honest. Any moment that left her breathless could eclipse the destitute landscape that was left when her world fell apart.

The Spanish kid had definitely done that last night, but even his unexpected skill combined with his youthful energy couldn't compare with the touch of Logan's lips against the inside of her wrist. How had he done that? It was like magic, seeping from the warmth of his lips into her veins. Like the impossible glow of a blue-white star in a glass.

Trying to erase the memory, she took a sip of the mimosa, savoring its sweet flavor on her tongue before swallowing. She closed her eyes. Logan wasn't a possibility in her life, even if she hadn't known him before. Sex was just a distraction. An exercise to avoid the darkness in her soul—not an all-consuming flame that might linger longer than the night.

Throbbing music began on the stereo. Rachel scanned the faces of the guests beginning to arrive. She spotted the Spanish kid. He was with a group of other young men, all splendidly godlike in their beauty. She didn't spare any of his companions a thought. Passion and beauty combined in the perfect combination only rarely. The Spanish kid was the exception that proved the rule. As if he felt her eyes on him, he glanced over.

She let her smile beckon him to her side.

Chapter 2

"Good morning, Logan." Tammy raised her eyebrows. "Good to see you. Here."

Logan looked up at the slight emphasis on the last word. Tammy stood beside the water cooler with a tall man he recognized vaguely from Accounts Payable. Glenn something. Both of them appeared bemused at his appearance, and he couldn't actually blame them, although no one but Tammy, who'd been his secretary since his days as a magician and his friend before he could afford to pay a secretary, would ever have mentioned it.

Logan preferred to take care of business anywhere but his office. Tammy, now his administrative assistant and second in command of his growing empire, had grown used to messengering files for his signature to whatever nook or cranny of the resort he'd adopted for the day. Sometimes it was the little coffee shop in the lobby of the hotel, but he'd been known to sit in one of the restaurants or lounges and take business calls from a back table. Once he'd driven a golf cart to a part of the course that was closed for maintenance and handled business calls there for a few hours.

Still, he had an office, and he needed to do some research on Rachel. She'd mentioned a divorce, but the changes in her seemed to indicate some hurt much deeper than a cheating husband. Whatever the answers were, the best place for this sort of inquiry was undoubtedly his office.

He waved her a half apologetic dismissal. "Just need a quiet spot for a while. You guys relax."

"Okay." Tammy and Glenn stepped aside as Logan entered his office. He switched on the laptop before he sat behind the desk and looked around. When was the last time he'd spent more than a few minutes in here? It could be seen as a waste of space. The office was large enough to house a conference table as well as his antique oak desk. Silvery vertical blinds masked the most glaring sunlight and real green plants flourished in the corners. It looked like the office of a successful businessman.

Not a has-been magician who's been trying to rewrite himself for the past few years.

A light tap on the door was followed by Tammy's frosted blonde head. "I brought you coffee."

"Thanks." He accepted the mug.

"Anything I can help you with?" She assumed an attentive pose but he sensed anxiety in her voice.

He smiled. "Everything's fine, Tammy."

"Did I ask? Of course everything's fine." She shrugged. "A little unusual, but fine. I have to admit I'm wondering what circumstance has forced you to take refuge in your office, though."

He leaned back in his chair, considering. Finally he made up his mind. "Rachel's here."

"Rachel?" She blinked, obviously not comprehending.

He made an impatient movement, scattering a few papers on his desk, then sank into the chair. "Rachel. Rachel. Nora's Rachel."

"Oh." Her face cleared, then she frowned. "Why?"

"Exactly." He sighed. "I haven't exactly kept up with her since Nora..." He trailed off, letting the last word expire in the silence even though it echoed in his heart. Died. He shook it off. "The last time I saw her was a few years ago. She'd come down to visit Jasmine at the same time I did. She was happy, I think, not much different from the last time I'd seen her with Nora. She and Jasmine had a great time. Blowing bubbles. Jazz loved it." He tried to imagine the sexy goddess he'd seen by the pool blowing bubbles with a toddler and found it impossible.

"This is not good." Tammy sounded almost angry. "What did she do? Come in here accusing you of something after all this time? You're not responsible for what happened to Nora, Logan."

Logan shook his head. "No, that's not it. Look, can you make a couple calls? Find out how she paid for the room? And how long she's staying."

Her frown deepened, but she nodded. "Fine."

After she left, Logan picked up the phone and dialed the poolside bar. Ramon answered. "S'up, man?"

"I want you to keep an eye on someone for me."

"Sure thing, boss." Ramon sounded as easy as if Logan had just asked him to make a Mai Tai.

"The woman I had you deliver the mimosa to. Rachel, a guest in suite 214."

"Will do my best, boss. Can barely see her through the crowd, though."

"Crowd?" Logan frowned.

"Yeah. Bunch of young studs." Ramon whistled softly. "Woman like that could eat any one of them alive, you ask me."

"Yeah. Thanks." Logan hung up as the door opened and Tammy came back in, a quizzical look on her face.

"Well, that was odd."

"What was odd?" Logan shook off the image of Rachel surrounded by attractive young men.

"Her name is Rachel Duvall, right? I did a little research and found she was using a credit card with a different name. Rachel Prescott. So I called the phone number she registered with and a woman answered. When I told her I just wanted to check on the validity of the card, she demanded to know where I was calling from. I told her, of course, thinking maybe the card was stolen. She said the card was fine, Rachel is her sister and she just got divorced so the credit card's under her married name."

"Okay. So?" Logan shrugged.

"Don't you think it's odd that her sister answered the number of the card's billing address?" Tammy raised her eyebrows.

Logan remembered Rachel's remark about her cheating husband getting her sister in the divorce. At first he'd thought she meant her sister had taken his side of the divorce, but maybe the betrayal had gone deeper than that. He decided it would be best not to mention his theory to Tammy, however. "Maybe they live together."

"And she didn't know where her sister was?" Tammy shook her head. "It just doesn't add up."

"Well, maybe someone else is worried about her." He said it almost to himself, wondering why it didn't make him feel better.

Tammy folded her arms over her chest and fixed him with an openly curious stare. "Which brings us to the million dollar question. Why are you so worried about her?"

The question made Logan pause. Tammy knew him better than almost anyone. They'd gone to high school together, had flirted but never dated. Logan had given her away at her wedding and was her son's godfather. Tammy, for her part, had been the one person Logan always knew he could count on. She'd been there when his life fell apart. She'd seen him through the worst and helped him achieve his best. When he moved to the Caribbean and asked her to go with him, she'd convinced her husband to uproot their family. Trent was no freeloader, and he hadn't been totally certain about giving up his life as an architect to take Logan up on his offer of designing and maintaining the resort's many buildings, walkways and outdoor venues.

He owed her an honest answer, but he wasn't sure...yet...if he had one, so he opted for the only reply he could offer. "I don't know."

She opened her mouth to say something else but before she could, a dark-haired man appeared in the doorway. "Hey, Logan. You busy?"

"Tony!" Glad for the distraction as well as the sight of his friend, Logan stood, a pleased grin on his face. "This is a surprise. Where's your lovely bride-to-be?"

"Downstairs with Andre and Stacey checking out the pool. The place has grown since I was last here." Tony's grasp was firm and he looked strong. Logan was sincerely happy for his friend, who'd fought addiction most of his life. Of course, keeping hold of Lady Lydia, Las Vegas's favorite escape artist, was enough of an addiction for any man.

"It'll be good to see Andre and Stacey again. They haven't been here since their honeymoon." Logan smiled at the memory. "I have never seen a couple more in love than those two. Not that I saw them much then. They kept room service very busy."

"They're just as sickening now as they were then." Tony's grin belied his words. "Especially now Stacey's expecting. Andre won't leave her side for a second."

Logan chuckled. "And I'm sure you and Lydia aren't 'sickening' at all, huh?" He stopped his friend's protest with a raised hand and a laugh. "Don't worry, I'll stand it somehow or other. But let's go see the others. I want to catch up on the news."

"Logan, we hadn't finished—" Tammy stepped in front of him.

"It can wait." He walked around her.

"Logan, if this is about Nora, I really think—"

"Tammy!" He paused, glancing over his shoulder at her. He had to remind himself that if anyone had a right to mention Nora's name, it was Tammy, but not in front of Tony, for God's sake. He took a deep breath and turned, taking her hands. "Thank you. For worrying about me. But it's not about Nora." Even though everything's about Nora. Damn her. "I'm fine, and I promise not to get into any trouble. Now, can I please go out and play, Mom?"

Tammy's brow crinkled with worry. He knew she saw through him. She knew his deep-seated need to rescue women in trouble, and she knew it all stemmed from Nora. His wife. The one woman he couldn't save. But she just shrugged, crossing her arms over her chest as she turned away. She didn't approve but she wasn't going to stop him. Logan turned back to Tony only to find his friend's expression now echoed Tammy's. "Jesus." Logan rolled his eyes and started for the office door.

Tony caught up to him outside. "What's going on?"

"Nothing." Logan glanced at his friend and stopped at the look of disbelief on Tony's face. "Okay. Yeah, there's something. Someone. Her name's Rachel and she was Nora's best friend. She's here, but she's—different from the way I remember her, and I don't know why."

"Different how?"

Logan hesitated, searching for a way to put it into words. "She's always been attractive, but she sort of faded into the background before. She wasn't like this. Now she's sort of...primal. I've seen women like her before. Sexy, but with a hard edge. That's not Rachel. She's changed."

"Are you sure it's not just your perception of her?" Tony held up his hands in self-defense when Logan swung around on him. "Just sayin'. You know, she was your wife's best friend. Maybe you're just seeing a different side to her. Maybe she seemed different before because she was off limits."

Gritting his teeth, Logan forced himself to consider the possibility, but it didn't feel right. "No. No, that's not right. She's still off limits." He wondered if it was true and found himself compelled to confess. "I'll admit she took my breath away. You don't see women like that often. But there's something else, too. Like she's broken or something."

"Broken how?" Tony motioned at a golf cart and Logan obediently got in.

He sighed, shaking his head as Tony climbed into the driver's seat and put the cart into reverse, starting toward the pool area. "I don't exactly know. She's not what you'd expect. Beautiful, intelligent." He shot his friend a look and waited for the shock his next words were sure to elicit. "Last night, I did a magic trick for her."

Tony's eyebrows shot up, but he didn't look judgmental. "Really? You haven't done magic in a while. Not in public, anyway."

"I know, but… She made me want to." He shrugged. "Not that it was all that appreciated."

Tony pretended to look outraged. "You're kidding. You were being all magical and she resisted you? Something's obviously wrong there."

Logan couldn't help smiling. "Well, at any rate, she left. She thanked me for the trick and left. Probably to go pick up some other guy. Ramon says she's surrounded by college kids now." He glared at his own hands, as if they were what had failed to impress Rachel.

"College kids?" Tony glanced at him. "She doesn't sound like your speed, man."

"That's just it. She's not the type who should be playing this game. Even if I didn't know her, I've been reading the women who come here long enough so I can tell you exactly who's looking for sex, who's looking for money, who's looking for life-long love. And she's not any of those."

"Then what's she looking for?"

"Destruction." The moment he said it, he knew it was true. "Hers. I think she's looking to hate herself."

"Jeez." Tony pulled the golf cart into a spot near the pool and turned to Logan. "Tammy was right, wasn't she? This is about Nora?"

He winced at the name, a heart-deep pain piercing his chest. "It's not about Nora."

"It's always about Nora, man. You've got to stop blaming yourself. It wasn't your fault, and there was nothing you could do about it."

"Yeah. I know that. It's not about that." Except it was, and he knew it. He hadn't been there to save Nora, but Rachel was something different entirely. He could still be there when she needed him. He could still save her.

****

I'm older than I thought I was. Rachel had grown tired of the boys clustered around her. Their posturing and her former paramour's possessive attitude both bored and exhausted her. She still couldn't remember his name, either.

43

I remember Logan's name. And the way his lips felt on her wrist. Sweat dribbled down her neck. The Spanish kid eyed a droplet hovering near her cleavage. He raised his eyes to hers and she knew exactly what he was thinking. If he were only ten years older she might have been thinking the same thing. She just wasn't drunk enough to think it now, and she was disgusted with herself that she had ever allowed herself to think it.

It was only mid afternoon, so the pool deck was crowded. Excusing herself, she made her way first to the restrooms and then slipped out on the other side. She'd left her bag behind, but she could get it later. She paused in front of the bar, scanning the other happy sunbathers. God, was everyone happy except her? Bitterness threatened to encroach on her, but she shoved it away. Bitterness did nothing but leave an aftertaste. She had no use for it.

As she thought this, her gaze was caught by Logan dressed in a white shirt and khaki shorts. He stood on the other side of the pool, shaking hands with a tall, good-looking, dark-haired man. As Rachel watched, he bent to kiss the cheek of a lovely woman in red with brown hair and another flame-haired woman dressed in a black sundress. Rachel wondered who these people were, but there was no way she was going to go ask. They belonged to a happier world, far away from where she existed. She watched for a moment as they chatted animatedly and laughed and another dark-haired man joined them.

It's a family. Rachel swallowed a bit of bile at the thought, but when the slight brown-haired woman turned and Rachel saw the beginnings of a pregnant belly, she swayed, her heart thudding in her throat.

"Are you all right?" A woman's startled voice beside her caught her off guard. She shot the unsuspecting blonde a glare dark enough to make her step back, but the next second others gathered around. Rachel tried to fend them off, but her defenses were too weak. Flashes of red and black overwhelmed her and she crumpled, her last thought that maybe—just maybe—she'd fall into the pool and the aching emptiness in her would fill with pool water and it would finally be over...

Her senses returned slowly. She felt strong arms around her, a stern voice giving orders. She knew who held her instinctively, without even opening her eyes. Logan. As if it had always been him. As if she'd never feel another man's arms around her again.

Maybe I won't. Her heart felt heavy and she let her head rest against his chest. At some point he put her down and covered her gently. She didn't open her eyes before the darkness enveloped her.

Chapter 3

Logan watched her wake slowly. In his semi-dark, cool office she blinked and rolled onto her side, sitting up. The blackness of her hair covered her face for a moment, but he sensed she knew where she was...or at least who she was with. He brushed her hair back from her face. "You have quite a fan club."

Rachel straightened, shaking her hair the rest of the way off her face, and the soft blanket he'd covered her with slid from her shoulders. "Do I?"

"Some kid keeps calling you his queen, if my Spanish doesn't fail me." He leaned forward, eyes on her face. "What happened?"

She shrugged. "Too much sun, I guess. Sorry, didn't mean to cause a fuss." Her eyes scanned the room curiously. "Where are we?"

"My office." He stood, crossing to the bar and pouring a glass of water from the crystal decanter. He returned to her, holding it out.

She accepted it, one eyebrow raised. "I knew you'd made good use of your time here, but now I'm beginning to see life has been very good to you."

"We both know that's not entirely true." He kept his voice bland. If she was trying to get a rise out of him, it was probably a defensive mechanism. He nodded to the glass in her hand. "Drink it."

She made a face. "Don't you have anything better to offer?"

He folded his arms over his chest. "You need to understand that if I hadn't already had a doctor in here to check your vitals, you'd be on a helicopter heading for the closest thing I could find to civilization. But he assured me you were all right...except for a slightly elevated level of alcohol in your system." He paused, his eyes on hers. "But I'm beginning to suspect the doctor isn't right at all about that."

She looked away, and he knew he'd hit a nerve. For whatever reason, this woman was far from all right, and the self-destructive path she'd chosen would consume her. And if it didn't do it fast enough for her, she'd finish the job. He couldn't let that happen. For her sake. For Nora's. For mine.

She cleared her throat, taking an obedient sip of the water. "I'm sorry. For what I said before. I know why you're here. I wish I knew why I am. I just...I got here and found you masquerading as a bartender and—"

"I'm not masquerading as anything." As he spoke, he realized it was the deepest lie he'd ever told. He'd been pretending to be something else since Nora's death. First he'd pretended he could carry on and then he'd pretended he wasn't a magician and now, in his own hotel, he was the biggest imposter of all. A man whose heart wasn't broken, a father who never missed his daughter, a widower who didn't grieve. And a magician with no real magic. He shook it off, redirecting the rising anger in his heart at her. "Who's the Spanish kid?"

"Some guy I picked up last night. Pretty good in the sack. " She gave him an arch look. "I guess at nineteen you were pretty inexhaustible, too."

An impossible urge to wipe that look off her face with a kiss almost overwhelmed him. He fought it off. If what she said was true, she needed his help more than he'd believed. "Did you forget we have a date tonight? You said it might be worth waiting for."

She stood, letting the blanket fall completely from her body, revealing tanned skin so perfect it took his breath away. Dear God, from the amount of sun-worshipping she did, she must have amazing genes. She stretched, cat-like, and turned back to him. "I've never been good at waiting."

For a moment he stood frozen. She's still off limits. He didn't want to give in to the desire, but he couldn't let her walk away. And she would. If he didn't make a move, she'd leave. The room, the island, probably his life. And she needed him, maybe as much as he needed her. He put his arm around her waist and snaked her close to him in a single movement, pausing to brush her hair back from her face. "Maybe it's time to stop waiting, then."

****

Her breath left her body the moment he pulled her into his arms. Had she wanted this from the start? Possibly. Seducing Nora's husband. The ultimate betrayal of herself and her old friend. It certainly would help further her self-hatred along its course. Dear God, he felt good. If only he didn't make her feel so alive. She hadn't counted on that.

Since Kevin's desertion, she'd reserved herself exclusively for the men who wanted nothing more than to use her to achieve something for themselves. Even the Spanish kid with his talk of "mi reina" was no better than most of them, although his youth at least gave him some excuse. But Logan. God, he was different. Had she ever felt like this? His gentle exploration of her mouth, the feel of his hand at the nape of her neck, his fingers in her hair. It was shared sensation, as if she could feel her own lips beneath his, capture his pleasure in the texture of her hair, breathe the very breath he did as he drew away.

Deep down she wanted to protest his withdrawal, but as he turned, she realized the door to his office had opened. One of the dark-haired men she'd seen Logan with earlier stood there. "Sorry, Logan. The doctor called. He wanted to make sure everything was okay."

The other dark-haired man slipped past the first, his sharp gaze taking in their embrace. Rachel could see the suspicion in his eyes, and she didn't blame him. What was he supposed to think after she'd passed out on the pool deck and was now found in a passionate moment with her rescuer? It sounded like a plot for a bad romantic comedy. Except there wasn't anything comedic about it. Was the pregnant brunette out there, too? Rachel stepped back from Logan, felt his grasp loosen reluctantly. "You have guests. I should go."

Logan gave her a glare that held her in place for a moment. "Why? Aren't you up for dinner tonight?"

No. I shouldn't be with you. You might actually be good for me and I can't risk that. She opened her mouth to say she couldn't make it, but the flame-haired woman from earlier entered.

"Did you say dinner?"

"I'm famished." And there she was. The beautiful, young pregnant woman. She smiled at Rachel, oblivious to the sharp pain her presence struck in Rachel's breast. "You look like you could use some food."

Logan rolled his eyes. "Rachel, this overbearing lot are my friends. Andre, Tony…" The two dark-haired men nodded. The sharp-eyed man was Tony. His brother Andre looked a little more relaxed. "…Andre's wife Stacey and Tony's fiancée Lydia. They decided to surprise me."

"N-nice to meet you." Rachel summoned a smile.

"Tony and Lydia are planning their wedding here this summer. They came down for one more look at the place—"

"And to help you celebrate." Stacey, her lovely face glowing with the unmistakable aura of imminent motherhood, reached out to take Logan's hand.

Rachel noticed Logan's wince, quickly covered by a smile. Curious, she tore her eyes away from Stacey. "Celebrate what?"

"My birthday." Logan spoke as if it were too difficult to open his mouth completely, his teeth slightly gritted.

"Oh." She recoiled. "You didn't mention that."

"I don't really celebrate it…anymore." Logan gave his friends a brief glance.

"Well, if you're going to start celebrating now, you don't want me around."

As she started to turn away, his hand caught hers. When she turned back, he spoke mildly, "You're wrong about that."

"Of course you are." Stacey stepped forward with a smile. Rachel couldn't help but notice that Lydia kept her distance, her arms folded over her breasts, her gaze slightly suspicious. But Stacey obviously had no qualms about the strange woman she'd just found in her friend's arms. "You really should join us for dinner. Especially if you and Logan had plans anyway."

"We didn't—"

"Yes. We did." Logan gave her a quelling look.

"Nothing absolute." She raised a hand as if to ward him off and he laughed.

"You're not getting out of it that easy." He bent his head to whisper in her ear, "You said I'd be worth waiting for. I intend to prove you right."

His lips brushed the skin beneath her ear and a tremble went through her. Maybe, just for tonight… She looked up at him, forgetting for a moment that they were surrounded by people of varying degrees of friendliness.

"I'm not taking no for an answer." He turned to the door again, pulling her along with him. A woman with frosted hair stepped back in surprise when the door opened. She held a robe and Logan took it smoothly. "Thank you, Tammy." He glanced over Rachel's head at his stunned friends. "I'm going to take Rachel back to her room. In spite of your surprise visit, your rooms should be ready by now, too." As he spoke, he deftly helped Rachel into the robe, even tying the belt loosely around her waist.

"They are." Tammy spoke with the competent air of a woman used to anticipating Logan's every request. "In the same building as—hers." Her voice faltered as if she couldn't quite decide what to call Rachel.

"Good." Logan took Rachel's hand again. "We'll meet you all by the pool after Rachel has a chance to shower." He waved over his shoulder and propelled Rachel outside.

Only when he had her seated in the golf cart did he release her. She gave him an amused look. "You're not used to people saying no to you, are you?"

He raised an eyebrow, giving her a half smile. "I'm not sure I know why anyone would want to. I'm always right."

She laughed at the outrageous statement but she noticed the slight touch of irony in his voice. Not only did he not believe he was always right, she wondered if he had any faith left in himself at all. *We're more alike than I thought. Nora's death obviously still weighed on him. The idea saddened her, and she quickly shook it off. If she started feeling sympathetic to him, she'd begin feeling sorry for herself and she'd sworn she'd never shed another tear.

"Why do you do that?" He glanced at her as he pulled onto the path.

"What?" She inspected her nails. She'd painted them red that morning and she was pretty sure they wouldn't chip so soon, but it gave her an excuse not to pay any attention to him.

"Put up that wall. You start to look almost human for an instant and then I blink and you're back to being a goddess again."

She smiled, looking at him from under her thick eyelashes, knowing she could seduce him just as she'd seduced so many other men. Lesser men and boys, yes, but he had the same foibles. She could do it. "You think I'm a goddess?"

"I think you're a woman." His firm voice jolted her into looking directly at him. Only when she bit her lip and turned away did he speak again, his voice softer. "A woman in pain."

If he only knew. She didn't look back at him, knowing her eyes would reveal too much at that moment. And if he knew, it would surely destroy her. She'd have to leave before he could find out. For the first time since her arrival, she began looking for an exit plan.

****

He endured the rest of the silent drive back to her room stoically, refusing to give in. He'd pierced the icy layer she shielded herself with, and he wasn't going to back down. During those moments he'd held her in his arms in his office, he'd sensed the woman she was, the woman she had been. That woman could love, she would cry and laugh a real, tender laugh.

That was the woman he wanted to know. The woman who was mind-blowingly sexy without barriers. The woman he'd only glimpsed for an instant since she came to the island. Tony was partly right, he suspected. His perception of Rachel had changed. She was different from what he remembered, but she wasn't letting him see the real woman at her core, either.

She's there, though. Maybe it would take more than a little magic to free her from whatever it was that haunted her. Whatever she was hiding from.

He pulled into a spot next to her building and they both sat still for several seconds. Finally she spoke. "I don't think I can be who you want me to be." Her voice almost sounded gentle.

"You already are." He reached for her hand, encouraged when she didn't pull away. "When I kiss you, that's who you are." She raised her gaze to his and he thought he saw a flicker of something there. He kissed her hand.

Her lips parted, but then she smiled and stepped out of the cart, lithe as a cat. "I don't know who you think I am, but it's not me. On the other hand, if you'd like to take me to dinner, I'm willing."

He got out of the cart. "Fine."

"What?" She scanned him. "You gonna wash my back?"

"I'm not letting you out of my sight." He brushed past her, leading the way into the building.

She laughed. "I can think of worse ways to shower." She paused, a frown creasing her forehead. "Damn. I left my bracelet thingy in my bag. By the pool."

"Not a problem." He produced the duplicate he'd already obtained. He'd had valet services retrieve her bag earlier and take it to her room.

"You do think of everything, don't you? And what luck. You're a bartender and I need a drink." She chortled, following him up the stairs to her room.

He doubted very much that she needed any such thing, but he didn't want to say that. Instead, he slid an arm around her waist and opened the door, half leading, half propelling her through the entrance. "What did you have in mind?" At her sly look, he added, "to drink?"

"Oh, you know what I like." She waved her hand and strolled across the floor, casually letting the robe slip from her shoulders as she ran the fingers of her right hand lightly across the back of the microsuede couch.

"Not really. I know you like mimosas." He moved into the kitchenette, opening the minibar door and surveying the contents.

"I like sex on the beach better."

He turned and caught her eye. The promise he read there made him smile a little in spite of himself. "Is that a suggestion?" He glanced at the minibar again. "I don't think I have all the ingredients."

She laughed. "Silly. We've got everything we need without anything in that little refrigerator." She stalked across the floor to him, running her hands over his chest and tilting her head as if to kiss him, but instead he felt the warm wetness of her tongue flick across his lips, tempting him to suck it into his mouth, to take possession of her...

He backed away, startled again by the pure animalistic passion she could raise in him. He'd spent the past few years of his life avoiding any relationship that could threaten his reserve, either emotionally or passionately, but this woman had broken through his defenses. And their past just complicated things. "My friends will be waiting for us."

"Not for at least an hour." She nipped at his neck. "Plenty of time. And then we'll both have what we really want and you can go on to dinner with them. No strings, I promise."

As she spoke, her hands moved to the waistband of his shorts, her touch on his skin mesmerizing, arousing and electrifying at the same time. But her words had already penetrated his consciousness. He seized her wrists, pulling away at the same time. "You think that's all I want from you. Sex."

She looked up at him, her eyes dark in the sunlight filtering through the sheer curtains. "It's all I have."

****

She could see the words shake him to his core. It was what she wanted. If he would leave her, it would make what she had to do that much easier. Leave. I'm not what you need, what you want. I can't be that person again.

I swore I'd never be that person. She hurts too much.

He took a step back, but his grasp on her hands never loosened. He shook his head. "I don't believe you."

"Dammit." She yanked her hands away from him, turning, her anger and near despair spilling over. "What the hell is wrong with you? Why? Why do you want to insist on

59

believing in me? You barely know me. Why can't you just fuck me and leave like the rest of them?"

He didn't flinch at her rude language, his face impassive. "That's what you want? You want me to make love to you?"

"No!" She gasped it, her breath short. Yes, God yes. She raised her hands to shove him away. "I said fuck me, not make love to me. You want me. You've wanted me since last night. You and your little magic trick. Trying to make me feel special. God!" She shoved him again, harder this time, and he surprised her by catching her around the waist and holding her against him. Images whirled through her head. Nora's face, the beautiful pregnant woman. Stacy. Nora's baby girl. Jasmine. A hand on a swelling belly, full of promises...but those promises had all been broken.

She tried to push him away, shaking her head. Something wet splashed against her arm and she froze, staring at it in shock. A low moan worked its way through her throat and escaped her mouth. Not this. Not the tears. Not the crying. The black hole yawned in her soul. In another moment it would engulf her. To stop herself from splitting apart, she wrapped her arms around herself and crumpled to the floor, escaping his grasp at last.

She felt him kneel beside her, and she struck out savagely, the tears nearly blinding her. "Get out! Get out, damn you. Just leave me alone." Just leave. You let her die. You let Nora die. Just go and let me be. Let me die…

God, yes. It was what she'd known would come for her sooner or later. The sweet desire for nothingness. To let it have her, this yawning blackness in her core. It was all that was left of her soul. It seemed only right to let it take her. If he would just leave she could do it, finally, be done with all of it. If she could just make him go, the sleeping pills were in her cosmetic bag. There were enough. And the alcohol in the minibar. She could make it a party.

The threat of heart-tearing sobs eased off and the blood stopped roaring in her ears. Maybe he was gone. Hopefully, she raised her head, her arms still wrapped around herself. As she did so, however, she felt his hands on the skin of her rib cage, helping her stand.

She looked at him wearily, too tired to fight him off any longer. Why won't he just leave? No longer considering what she was doing, she touched his face, letting her fingertips enjoy the smooth surface. She sighed. "I guess you of all people know what it's like. To lose something. Permanently, I mean. Something you treasured more than anything and you realize all of a sudden that it's gone."

****

He almost recoiled at her statement but caught himself just in time. His heart ached for her. And for Nora, his dead wife. And Jasmine, his motherless daughter. He remained silent, hoping if she would just tell him what pain had brought her to this state, he'd be able to help her. Because if there was one thing he knew, it was pain. And guilt.

Her voice fell into his silence. "It was like that. Like losing the watch my grandmother gave me when I was at college. The moment I realized it was gone. The hours I spent retracing my steps and calling my friends and the frustration of knowing I'd just had it...I put it on my wrist that morning. And somehow it was gone."

Her eyes took on a faraway look. "Then there's the moment when you've exhausted every possibility and you realize...it's just gone. The thing you loved and cherished and valued and thought you'd have forever is gone and it's all your fault. And it's late at night and you have to sleep and you know that when you wake up, it'll still be gone." Her voice faded a little. "Just gone." She leaned her head against his chest. "You do know what that's like, don't you?"

He did know. With stunning clarity and unhinging certainty, he knew. And though he longed to know what precious thing she'd lost to bring her to this state, he didn't ask.

She would tell him eventually, but he couldn't ask. "No one's called me Ian since she died." When she looked at him questioningly, he added, "Nora. You know that, though. After she died, I told everyone to call me Logan, but I didn't say why." He drew in a deep breath. "It's because it was the last word she ever said to me. I called her and she put up the usual good front, telling me all the things I wanted to hear. The baby was fine, she was fine. I was in a hurry, so that was all I heard. I had to get onstage. I said good-bye, but just as I was about to hang up, I heard her say my name."

He broke off, the pain on his face apparent. "I hung up. I had to get to the show. I told myself that whatever it was she'd thought of, it could wait. I was wrong. And after that, I couldn't stand to hear anyone else say my name." He lowered his gaze. "I know it was my fault. If I had just stopped a second to listen, if I'd just let her know I was there for her. Hell, I don't even know where I was. Vegas, Los Angeles, New York. Wherever my next gig was." He sighed. "She had to do it all alone. She had the baby while I was on stage. I called her between shows. I went home the next day, helped her bring the baby home, got them settled and flew back. Never missed a show."

He led her to the couch and sat, pulling her with him. He could smell the salty scent of her dried sweat in her hair. She smelled like the beach he'd come to love. He caressed her arm, feeling the light hairs beneath his palm. He kissed her forehead when she looked up at him. He could take her to the bedroom and make love to her. She wouldn't fight him anymore and he could bury the rest of the story he never wanted to tell in the pleasure of holding her.

"Logan?"

Her voice broke into his pleasant musings, bringing him back to the reality of what he'd already confessed to the woman he wanted to save. Her eyes were red, but they'd lost their detached look. She wanted him to finish the story. He kissed her forehead and released her, sitting up. "I didn't miss a show. What I missed was that my wife felt displaced in the big house I bought for us in California. After her mother left, she was alone, coping with the biggest change she'd ever experienced. And I was in Vegas, performing magic, working on my career. I never missed a show, but I missed the fact that my wife was depressed. The signs I saw I chalked up to baby blues of a first time mother, not post-partum depression. And then she was gone."

He met her gaze. "So yeah. I know what it's like to lose something."

"I'm sorry, Logan." Her voice trembled a little, and she cleared her throat. "You can't take all the blame, though. I was there, too. I spent a week with her. Her mother and her sister, too. We all missed it. Maybe it wasn't that obvious."

"At least you were there." He glanced over at her. "I wasn't. I knew her best, and if I had been there with her where I should have been as her husband, or just listened while I had the chance..." He shrugged. "Well, maybe it'd be a different story."

"Is that why you're so determined to save me?" Her lips curved in a soulless smile.

Is that what I'm doing? Saving you? Or redeeming myself? He turned toward her. "Maybe. I see the signs I missed with her."

"What signs?" She stood, pacing restlessly to the other side of the room, pausing by the minibar and pulling out a tiny bottle of wine. She held it up. "Sangria. Want to share?"

"Not much there." He stretched his legs out. How exactly had they gotten to this point? From her raging despair to his confession to a sudden friendly détente. Yet it felt like a normal progression. Like it was meant to be.

She glanced at her watch. "We're going to be late if you wait for me."

"I'll call Tony. We'll meet them at the restaurant." He appeared unconcerned.

She set the small bottle aside. "You're not going to let me out of this, are you? Why can't you just accept that I'm not worth saving?"

"Because I don't believe it." He pulled out his phone and began punching buttons, scrolling through emails. "I've known you a long time."

"Not really. Nora knew me. And you definitely don't know me now."

"Fine." He set the phone aside. "Then tell me. What changed? Why don't I know you now?"

She bit her lip, looking away. "I'm not ready to tell you that." Her face crimsoned as if in shame.

He nodded. "Then I'm not leaving you alone."

She stood for a moment, looking indecisive. Finally she broke the silence. "I'm going to take a shower."

"I'll be here." He picked up his phone again, pretending to check emails until he heard the shower start. Then he dialed Tony's number.

"Logan. Everything okay?" The anxiety in his friend's voice might have made Logan feel guilty if a sense of inevitability hadn't pervaded him so thoroughly.

"Yeah. Everything's fine, but we're running late. Rachel was a little more—" messed up "—exhausted than I'd taken into consideration. Go on to the restaurant. Ramon knows you're coming. Enjoy a few drinks and an appetizer. We'll be there as soon as possible."

"Okay, man. See you in a while." Tony's easy acquiescence filled Logan with gratitude. He hoped it meant his friends had decided to support him, even if they didn't agree with him. He'd noticed Tony's cautious attitude earlier. And forget Lydia or Stacey. They were so obviously suspicious of Rachel it was no wonder she'd broken down after meeting them.

But that wasn't fair, either. Lydia had been his friend for a long time, and Stacey was easily one of the fairest, most intelligent women he'd ever met. If these women were apprehensive of Rachel's motives, they were just trying to protect him. Logan focused on gratitude for his friends. "Yeah. Thanks."

He hung up and sat looking at his phone for a moment, lost in thoughts about his friends, his wife, the woman behind the bathroom door. Who would emerge from the shower, anyway? Would it be the real woman with the mysteriously broken heart or the sexy nymphomaniac with the fine sheen of diamond-like armor guarding her heart? And which would be easier to deal with?

Chapter 4

Rachel studied her reflection in the mirror for several minutes after her shower. Her first impulse was to apply the makeup she'd adopted recently. Bright lipstick, brazen blush, heavy mascara—a mask intended to hold others at a distance. Something about it didn't seem right, though. Instead, she contented herself with a little concealer to mask the shadows of sorrow under her eyes, a softer reddish-pink lipstick and just a little eyeshadow and mascara. She studied the result in the mirror. Not quite the almost-soccer mom she'd previously been. A little sexier, but not nearly the woman who'd lured a young Spanish stud into her bed.

Great. Now how do I dress? She studied the sundresses in her closet. She'd purchased most of them for the trip. They were nowhere near what she'd have worn before—before everything fell apart. Not that she wanted that, anyway. Her eye fell on a white dress buried in all the bright colors. White. The color of virgins. The color of mourning. Strange that the two shared something. She touched the dress and something about her red fingernails against the purity of the fabric pleased her. She pulled it over her head and studied herself in the mirror, arranging the light off-the-shoulder ruffle. If she pulled her black hair into a side ponytail and bound it with the pearl band from her wedding, the simplicity would suit the cut and color of the dress while providing dramatic contrast.

Taking a deep breath, she turned toward the door. She hadn't anticipated meeting Logan's friends, let alone spending the evening with them. She wished she could be alone with Logan, preferably behind closed doors. But then she hadn't anticipated his charged confession, her own inadequate attempt to ward him off, the amazing kisses and caresses they'd shared.

A light knock on the door startled her and she turned. "Come in."

Logan opened the door but didn't cross the threshold. He surveyed her with satisfaction. "You look better."

"Do I?" She took a step toward him and he produced a rose, seemingly from thin air. She paused, a smile making its way onto her face. "You're determined to make me believe, aren't you? Why is that so important to you?"

"It's not important to me, in particular. But if you don't believe in magic, it's hard to face life, isn't it? Some things you just have to take on faith." He brushed the rose against her cheek before handing it to her. "If you don't have faith, you don't have much to live for." He turned his hands over and back again, put them together and pulled them apart with a flourish that produced another rose, white this time. He held it out to her with a little bow.

She took the rose, placing it against the first, a study in white and red. Faith seemed a long way from the life she'd led for the past few months. Since Kevin. She steeled herself for the sharp pain of betrayal and loss at the thought of her ex-husband, but it didn't come.

She thought of the call from Angela. Her sister had sounded honestly worried about her, and a faint stirring of emotion made her frown. I never planned to forgive her. Or him, for that matter. What they did was unforgivable.

But then, too, she'd made them pay. Him, anyway. Kevin, a successful criminal lawyer, should have been living in a mansion with every comfort life could offer him. Instead he was shacked up with her sister in a tiny two-bedroom condo, half of his income earmarked for alimony, most of his possessions gone now and the four bedroom, three-and-a-half bath brick home on the river—his dream house—closed up until she chose to come home. If she ever did.

Yeah, she'd won that court battle.

At one time, the thought had brought her some measure of satisfaction, but now it fed the darkness inside her, just as the sexy young men had done. She didn't want to think about the darkness anymore. She buried her nose in the scent of the roses and closed her eyes, searching for faith. A tiny blue-white light. She smiled a little. Whatever she'd done right or wrong, that moment when she'd held a star certainly tried to brighten even the dark corners of her soul.

But can it? Really? The answer came almost instantly. Only if you believe it can.

She opened her eyes and met his gaze. Only inches apart, she could feel the heat of his body. Just an hour before, she would have welcomed this proximity but in her current vulnerable state she found herself backing away. "What's for dinner?"

Taking the hint, he straightened and took a step back. "I'm actually pretty proud of that, actually, and I'm going to keep it a secret." He grinned. "Fortunately for my friends, I was already planning to impress you, so they get an opportunity to see my latest creation, too."

"Well, now I am intrigued." She set the roses aside and took his arm. "Won't you show me?"

She was a little surprised when he didn't lead her to the parking lot for a golf cart. Instead he chose one of the paths to the beach. She paused at the end of the boardwalk. "Um, is this a long walk?"

He glanced down at her feet. "High heels? Who wears high heels to the beach?"

"Well, if you'd mentioned that your latest invention—"

"Creation."

"—involved a hike on the beach, I might have opted for more appropriate footwear." She surveyed the sandy shoreline in despair.

He laughed. "No worries. Take 'em off." To illustrate, he kicked off his own loafers, leaving them by the steps.

"Those look expensive."

"Nobody'll take them." He bent, taking first one foot, then the other and slipping her high-heeled sandals from her feet with expert fingers.

She shivered a little at the contact of his fingers against the sensitive skin of her calf, but when he glanced up, she flashed him an unconcerned smile. "Okay, but if my Jimmy Choos get washed out to sea, you're buying me another pair." She sighed in contentment. "I have to admit, that does feel better." She grinned at him. "Not that a man could understand."

"There's nothing like the feel of sand between your toes. That I do understand."

She glanced sideways at him, unable to contain a little smile. She couldn't even remember what he'd been like back in his heyday as a magician. She'd only seen him a few times, and those had been with a lot of other people. Usually at a dinner or party or something Nora had set up.

Nora wasn't hard to remember, though. Rachel remembered feeling her friend was all grown up, throwing dinner parties, married to a wildly handsome and successful man. She was a far cry from the wild child of their teenage and college years. But she'd always seemed happy, and for the life of her, Rachel couldn't find it in herself to understand what had happened to change that. Not really. If anything, Nora's was a life to envy. Beautiful home, new baby. During the time Rachel had spent with her friend after Jasmine's birth, Nora had seemed quieter than usual but not especially sad. Tired and maybe a little wistful when she held the baby, but not depressed.

And Logan still blamed himself. One memory stood out clearly in Rachel's mind from that time. His face when he came home. The grief and guilt in his eyes when he took baby Jasmine from her grandmother's arms. He'd just stood there for several minutes in the midst of the knot of people who'd loved Nora so much and waited for him to comfort them. And then he'd handed the baby back to Nora's mother and dropped into a chair, covering his face.

Rachel could still see that man in the one beside her. But not the magician, at least not the stage magician he'd been. The grand illusionist whose shows had entertained and charmed thousands, whose career had been on the fast track to Hollywood and beyond. Yet she had a feeling that if she let herself he could make her believe in magic.

Her toe stubbed on something in the sand and he caught her arm to steady her. "Sorry. Are you tired?"

"No. Just—" She looked around, realizing how far they'd walked. "Are you sure we're going in the right direction?"

He flashed her a grin that reminded her a little of the man he'd once been. "Pretty sure." He pointed to a dune that jutted out a little further than the others. "It's just around that bend."

"Okay, but my pedicure won't be the same after this." She let him tuck her hand through his arm, glad for the support as they resumed the trek.

Sure enough as they approached the dune, she heard music and laughter, and when they rounded the bend, she stopped short in amazement. Light spilled out from the little beach bar onto the sand. "You built this?" She glanced over her shoulder. At his pleased nod, she added, "It's beautiful."

It was. The roof was covered in real thatched straw, but she suspected it had better roofing material beneath. Three sides were open to the lovely night breezes, but she could see glass doors folded back against the sturdy wooden posts at each corner. The third side was solid with swinging doors that led into the kitchen. A bar faced forward toward the ocean and was decorated with lights of every color. Colored lights in the corners of the bar and tiki torches around a patio with a fire pit completed the oasis of light on the dark beach. Rachel thought the effect of the warm firelight and the colored lights combined in a way that reminded her of the "star" she'd held in the glass. Was that just last night?

The laughter was coming from the patio around the fire and Logan led Rachel to the small group gathered there. "Logan!" Stacey stood at his approach. "This is wonderful. I'm so glad we get a chance to see it first."

"You've outdone yourself this time, my friend." Andre shook Logan's hand. "This place will be in every guidebook by the end of the year, I predict."

"What are you calling it?" Lydia asked the question Rachel realized she'd wanted to ask all along.

"I've considered several names." Logan stepped behind the bar, surveying his friends' drinks. Rachel noticed that he poured both Stacey and Tony fresh club soda before producing a pitcher of Sangria and pouring some for the rest of them. As he handed her a glass, he added, "I thought maybe you could help." His smile felt like it was all for her, but then he turned and addressed the rest, "Suggestions?"

Everyone seemed up for the challenge. By the time a pretty young waitress delivered the fish tacos, Stacey had suggested La Joya or The Jewel, Lydia opted for Arena Pura (Pure Sand), and Tony and Andre were arguing over Hermosa Vista or Vista Linda as a tribute to the beautiful view. Of the suggested names, Lydia leaned toward Stacey's tribute to the jewel-like light.

"You haven't said much, " Andre smiled at her. "Any opinion?"

She opened her mouth to say she felt La Joya would be perfect but hesitated, glancing at Logan, who leaned on the bar, his expression noncommittal. "What about Estrella de Mar?"

"Sea Star." Logan nodded with a little smile. "I like that."

"It's perfect." Stacey's smile warmed Rachel almost as much as Logan's. She smiled back while the others murmured assent.

"That's it then." Before anyone could react, Logan pulled out a bottle of club soda and poured champagne glasses full of it. "I hereby christen this bar Estrella de Mar."

They all drank solemnly, then Lydia turned her unsettling green eyes on Rachel. "So what made you think of that name? Not that it's not perfect, but I get the feeling there's more to the story."

"It was...something Logan showed me." Rachel shot him a glance and found herself ensnared by his gaze, suddenly too intense to look away from. Only when Andre cleared his throat did she remember that there were others in the room and she quickly redirected the question. "Which reminds me. The island's name. Isla Foriscura. I've looked it up but I can't find a meaning."

"Excellent question." Andre turned to their host, raising his eyebrows questioningly. "I've often wondered the same thing. Where did the name come from?"

"The name came with the island, actually. It's been called that for centuries. I asked around a little on the mainland once, and close as I can get, it's Latin." Logan leaned on the bar, looking mysterious. "And it comes with a story."

"Well, don't keep us in suspense. Latin for what?" Tony set his glass on the bar.

"And the story, please." Rachel spoke without thought, but her words brought an approving smile from Logan. He'd obviously been waiting to be asked.

"Let's go outside if you want the story." Logan beckoned them to the table set with their dinner. Only after they were seated did he continue. "The name means, literally, 'outdoor cure'. Foris is the latin word for outdoors and 'cura' evidently comes from the Latin word curatio for cure. The story is that after the fall of the empire, a Roman soldier came here. He was wounded and weary from his travels and the war, and he thought he was looking for a place to die in peace. The locals took a liking to the man, so they helped him reach this island, set him up with food and a temporary shelter, tended his wounds and left him. They thought he would die peacefully after settling up with his gods because, as the story goes, infection had set in and he was near death. A week later, a man from the village came to bury the soldier, but what he found wasn't a corpse. The soldier, instead, had recovered completely and was fishing and hunting. Supposedly the soldier refused to leave his new island home except to trade in the village and he eventually married one of the native women and brought her here to live."

"That's why you came here." Rachel had been so drawn into his story she had almost forgotten where they were.

Logan focused on her. His words were simple. "No. It is why I stayed here, though."

"And bought the island and started one of the most popular resorts off the coast of Cancun. Yadi yada." Tony waved his hand as if to dismiss the story.

Lydia swatted his hand down. "Don't be a dick." At his hurt look, she smirked. "My love."

"Whatever. Just trying to lighten the mood." Tony leaned over and kissed his fiancée lightly.

Kevin had never done that. Not in a group. Rachel felt an odd yearning for that sort of intimacy. The kind that didn't care who was watching. What the hell brought that on? She stood, swayed, off-balance for some reason that had nothing to do with the sangria.

Logan stood, too. "You okay?"

She nodded, mute for a moment, finally finding words. An excuse and an escape all in one. "The, um, bathroom?" She looked at him appealingly. Please let me go.

"In the back." His furrowed brow indicated he'd picked up on something else in her voice. She nodded, stumbling away.

In the bathroom—a spotless black and white marble room that contrasted nicely with the bar's overall rustic appearance—she leaned on the sink for a moment, feeling giddy and a little sick. What's wrong with me? She remembered the concern in Logan's voice, the way he'd caught her arm to steady her and her stomach did another flip that didn't bode well for the fish tacos.

But she wasn't sick. She knew she wasn't, just as she knew this feeling went beyond the shared desire and kisses she and Logan had already experienced. She didn't just like Logan.

She wasn't just attracted to him. She suspected she could fall in love with him, and that was more than she'd counted on. Cold from the floor seeped through her bare feet and into the pit of her stomach.

The bathroom door opened and Stacey entered. "Hey, sorry. I swear, I think my bladder's shrinking with every ounce this kid gains."

Rachel laughed. "No worries. I was the same way when—" She stopped herself from finishing the sentence, pain stunning her like a slap across her face. When I was pregnant. Had she actually gotten so complacent with these people—with Logan—she'd forgotten? She couldn't allow that, could never excuse herself from the guilt and the pain.

Stacey came out of the stall and washed her hands at the sink next to Rachel. She didn't appear to have noticed the hesitation in Rachel's conversation. "At least I'm past the constant nausea. A month ago I wouldn't have been able to face those fish tacos, but I'm fine with it now, thank God."

"Those were great, weren't they?' Summoning all her strength, Rachel faced the other woman's pregnant glow and pasted a smile on her face. "I've heard the second trimester is the most fun. Have you felt the baby move yet?"

"Just a little here and there." Stacey's expression softened. "He's been kicking around a little tonight, actually.

Here..." She took Rachel's hand and placed it on her rounded belly.

Rachel refrained from pulling away with difficulty. She bent her head so the other woman couldn't see her face, focusing on her hand and remembering placing it on her own belly... She gasped at the unexpectedly strong kick, undeniable as an electric shock, and allowed herself the relief of yanking her hand away. Summoning her smile again, she said, "He's strong. I didn't think you'd be able to feel it so early."

"Well, I am five months along, so he better be getting strong." Stacey rubbed her belly again and then laughed. "I'm sorry. I've been rattling on for at least ten minutes about him, haven't I? Andre swears I can't talk about anything else and Lydia just gets bored by the whole thing. I'm sure she'll think different when it's her turn."

"I'm sure she will." Rachel turned under pretense of checking her makeup, got control of her churning emotions and returned her attention to Stacey. "We should get back, though. Only..." she hesitated, then plunged on. "Just enjoy this. All of it." Her lips quirked in the first sincere attempt at a smile of the evening, and it felt as if it were on crooked.

Stacey gave her a curious look, then took her hand impulsively. "I am."

"Good." The word choked out of her throat and Rachel fled.

****

"So you really believe this place has some sort of magical healing powers?" Andre leaned on the bar across from where Logan was polishing the glasses he'd just washed. Tony and Lydia had disappeared into the back and Stacey and Rachel were still in the bathroom.

Logan didn't answer until he'd finished the last glass and put it away. Then he turned to his friend, flipping the towel over his shoulder. "I believed it enough to start this place. I hoped it would help more people than just me." He thought of Rachel and almost sighed. Every time he thought the magic of the island might help her heal, she pulled away. He'd seen it in her eyes when she went to the bathroom. His story about the island had brought her just a little too close to believing.

He heard the bathroom door open and saw Rachel coming toward him, her eyes a little too bright. She looked so vulnerable in her white sundress and bare feet. He wanted to take her in his arms and hold her until she was ready to trust him with whatever sorrow burdened her.

A few more days. She'll be okay if she stays here a few more days. I'll wear her down and she'll tell me about it and then the healing can begin.

She started toward him, and he suspected she was going to ask him to take her back to her room. He was ready to oblige, but just as she reached the bar, Stacey came out of the bathroom and the kitchen door opened, spilling out Tony and Lydia as well as several of the kitchen staff, Ramon and Tammy carrying a large birthday cake. Without pausing to think what he was doing, Logan reached across the bar and caught Rachel's hand as his other friends closed in around them to sing "Happy Birthday."

He managed to keep hold of her while he came around the bar to stand next to her. Just from the light touch of their hands and where their shoulders brushed he could feel how tightly coiled she was. As the last notes of the song died away and he blew the candles out, she gave his hand a squeeze and kissed his cheek. But then she pulled away and in the press of congratulations from his friends and co-workers, he lost sight of her.

What had begun as an intimate dinner party with a few friends had become an all-out birthday blast. And though he'd made it a point not to celebrate his birthday since Nora's death, he couldn't find it in his heart to resent his friends. Not even

Tammy, who'd probably orchestrated the whole thing. But this was not what Rachel needed and certainly not what he'd had planned for the evening.

He gritted his teeth until everyone had their cake and a glass of champagne in hand. Only then did he search for Rachel. She stood at the edge of the light, half-turned away, her arm held by Stacey, who looked anxious. Rachel shook her head, her raven hair falling over her shoulders. When had she released it from its ponytail? Not that it mattered. Logan started toward her, but before he could take more than a step, she glanced his way and pulled her arm from Stacey's grasp in the same moment. She backed away, saying something to Stacey, her eyes still on Logan. She shook her head, turned and fled.

Logan hurried to Stacey. "What did she say?"

"Just to tell you she was sorry, she couldn't stay." Stacey looked troubled as she turned to him. "And that she can't believe anymore. Logan, what's wrong with her?"

"I wish to God I knew." Logan drew her into a quick reassuring embrace. "But I promise I won't let her leave until I find out."

He forced himself to relax as he worked his way back through the little crowd to speak to Andre and Tony. She couldn't leave the island tonight. Not without someone informing him, anyway. There was a small flight coming in but none scheduled to leave. So she had to go back to her room.

Unless she finds the Spanish kid. Or somebody like him. Or somebody worse. The thought sent a stab of worry and jealousy through him. He caught Andre's arm and pulled him aside. "I've got to go."

"Okay, but why?" Andre looked confused. "Is it Rachel? Are you sure about her, man?"

"I'm sure." The urgency in his chest increased and he started to turn when Andre caught his arm. He stopped, prepared to yank away from his friend if he had to, but he caught a look of concern on his friend's face.

"Let him go." Stacey's voice caught their attention and they both looked at her. She stepped forward. "I don't know what's wrong with her, but Rachel needs you right now, Logan."

Logan nodded. "You guys stay. Enjoy. And don't even think about asking for the bill, Andre. It's on me."

With that parting shot, he practically ran from the bar, hurrying to retrace the steps he'd walked so leisurely with Rachel earlier. Her sandals were gone. He wasn't sure if that was a good sign or not, but surely she'd want another shower before going to a bar. Her room must be the first place he tried.

She answered his knock calmly. "I'm sorry I left."

"You're sorry?" He stared at her, taking in her disheveled hair, her still bare feet, her rumpled dress. Without thinking, just happy he hadn't found her at the bar or in the embrace of another man already, he put his arms around her waist and stepped inside, kicking the door shut behind him.

For a long moment he just held her, his lips against her hair, breathing her scent, but when her arms looped around his neck in a motion suggestive of surrender, he turned his head, capturing her lips with his. God, had anything ever felt more right than this? He adjusted his stance to accommodate her shorter stature, hands still on her waist. He felt her hand in his hair, her lips open beneath his, her tongue velvety soft against his...

He needed to slow things down and find out why she'd run, but somehow he lost track of that in his desire to take her to the bedroom and know every inch of her, to hear her cries of fulfillment even before he took her...

"God." He gasped the one word prayer for strength and wrenched himself away. He took a deep breath. "Not yet."

"Why the hell not?" Although the words were confrontational, her tone was more amused. He took encouragement from it.

"You said you don't believe in magic. Would you believe in magic if you could do it?"

"For an ex-magician, you're very mysterious. I can't do magic tricks."

"Anyone can do magic." He took both her hands. "I see it every day."

A strange expression flickered over her face. Desire, hope and lingering cynicism seemed to war for control. She sighed. "I wish I could believe that." She glanced at the roses in the bud vase on her table, then back at him. "Fine, tell me how to do the trick with the star."

He shook his head. "That I can't tell you. And why not the rose? It's a pretty cool effect, I think."

"Not as cool as the star." She indicated the rose. "Although the rose is very impressive. Elegant."

He nodded. "Exactly. Elegant in its simplicity."

She frowned, spreading her hands. "Okay, I get that you want me to believe in magic. But why is it so important to you? What's your point?"

He met her gaze. "My point is, you're not asking me about the rose because you don't feel threatened by it. You've seen the effect a thousand times. It's a good one, especially when it's done well, but you're not concerned it'll make you believe in magic. The star on the other hand…" He shrugged. "If I tell you there's a trick behind that one, you may never believe."

"If I don't want to believe in magic, isn't that my business?" Her expression clouded.

He nodded. "That's true. But it's not my business to give you the fuel you need to not believe."

She tilted her head, an interested look on her face. "But you are in the business of helping people believe."

He hesitated, struck by her words and how close he'd come to saying the same thing. When exactly had he gotten back into that business?

She interrupted his ruminations. "I still want to know about the star, though."

"I tell you what, I'll do it again for you and if you can figure it out, I'll tell you if you're right."

"What? Right now?" She looked startled.

"Right now." He glanced over his shoulder. "It's dark. Should be a star or two if we go out on the balcony." He picked up an empty wineglass and held it out. "Well?"

Her chin tilted up at the challenge, and when she reached for the glass her fingers brushed his. He wondered if he'd made a mistake. If any woman could ever learn all his tricks, it was surely this one. But he also knew he wanted to try, and he had the definite impression that this might be the most important trick he'd ever done.

Chapter 5

Rachel hesitated at the doors leading out onto her private deck. "Don't you need to do some sort of, I don't know, preparation or something?"

He laughed at her, his eyes dancing. "What? You mean for the trick? I'll tell you a secret." He brushed her hair back and leaned over, his lips close to her ear. "Real magicians never have to prepare—as far as you know."

A pleasant shiver went through her. A vague memory stirred. Her mother in the kitchen preparing for a dinner party. A good hostess has all her preparation done before the party so it looks like she gets to enjoy everything as much as her guests. She pushed the memory away, knowing it would lead to others where she was the perfect hostess with everything prepared ahead of time. She'd already broken her vow never to cry again once that day. She steeled herself against doing it again.

Lifting her chin, she stepped past him onto the deck. Her hands gripped the white-painted wrought iron railing. His body was solid and warm behind her, but she clung to the cold metal rail as if to keep herself from flying up into the stars. She felt almost certain whatever he was about to do—whatever she was about to see—would surely turn her world upside down.

The tropical sun had set long before. She wondered what time it actually was but didn't really care enough to find out. Diamonds peppered the velvety black sky, and he wanted her to pick one. She lifted her hand and pointed. "That one."

He rested his chin on her shoulder, bending his legs so his tall frame molded against hers. She watched his hand the entire time as he reached past her arm, closed his long fingers and brought them back to the glass, releasing the light into the bowl of the wineglass. She stared in wonder at the blue light.

"Did you see a trick?" He smiled at her, offering her the glass, his hand still firmly on top of it.

She shook her head, not in denial but because she didn't want to take the glass. She'd have to let go of the railing and then she'd have no choice but to surrender.

His eyes narrowed and he lifted the glass with the hand covering the top. He considered the pinpoint of light for a moment, then drew his other hand in front, blocking the light from her eyes for a second. When he removed his hand, the light was gone, but he reached inside, then held his hand out, palm up. A diamond-like crystal winked at her. She wanted to believe it was the star.

And why couldn't she? If he wanted to give her the stars, why couldn't she just let him?

Her heart squeezed in her chest in a peculiar fashion she hadn't expected. She drew in a sharp breath. "Oh God."

"Are you all right?" His expression changed from triumph to concern.

"I'm—" not. And I don't think I ever will be again. She accepted the crystal and let go of the railing at the same moment, looking at him. "Don't leave tonight."

"That was never my plan."

Her heart pounded in her chest and she tried to come up with a sexy retort, but the emotions of the afternoon got in the way. Instead, she met his gaze with more sincerity than she'd allowed herself to show a man in months. She wanted him to kiss her, her body thrummed in time with his. And she knew her gaze told him that.

Nodding as if satisfied, he finally lowered his lips to hers, releasing her chin to put both hands on her hips and mold her to him, compensating for the several inches height difference with the ease of a tall man who had kissed many women. Her body tingled where he touched it, and when he moved his hands from her waist to the bare skin of her arms, beginning to taper off the kiss, she moaned softly. "Don't stop now."

He laughed, drawing away just enough to look down at her. "You taste so damn sweet."

Her body ached and she slipped her arms around his neck, not letting him move away. If he left her now, the temporary thaw of her heart might refreeze, leaving her incapable of ever feeling this way again. "Then don't stop." She breathed the words against his ear, feeling him tremble a little when she nipped at his earlobe. A heavy feeling of arousal weighed her middle. God, she wanted him. And he wanted her, too. In that moment, it was all that mattered.

****

She'd come to life in his arms as certainly as if he'd conjured her up, but the woman he held wasn't an illusion. Partly the sweet and vulnerable woman he'd known once as his wife's best friend, partly the sexy goddess he'd become acquainted with since she'd come to the island, this Rachel embodied everything he could ever have desired in a woman. And now that he finally had her, he never wanted to let her go. He kissed her neck just below her ear, his fingers sliding under the straps of her sundress, pushing them down her shoulders as he followed his gentle touch with a trail of kisses...

"God yes." She breathed the words, and he wasn't sure if she was answering a question or urging him to continue, but it didn't matter anymore, and he had no intention of stopping to ask…

"Rachel!" The sharp female voice made him start back. He turned his head, confused to find a young dark-haired woman standing at the open sliding glass door. She resembled Rachel enough to make him look twice. A little rounder, a little softer, not so breakable. This woman looked like she could bounce, and she was obviously used to being in charge. She hurried forward, grasping Rachel's arm and pulling her away.

"Jesus!" Rachel glared. "What the hell?" She stopped at the sight of the other woman's face. "Angel?"

Angel pulled Rachel into a firm embrace, fixing Logan with a reproving glare. "Oh, honey, I've missed you so much. You should never have left us like that."

"Left you?" Rachel looked stunned. "You—God, Angel, what the hell are you doing here?"

"I'm bringing you home. You shouldn't have left." She shot Logan another look, then turned her back on him, dismissing him. She brushed Rachel's hair back. "You've been living the wrong kind of life. You can't keep up this way. You can't just go around sleeping with any good-looking guy you happen across. God. What kind of diseases have you caught already?"

Logan looked from one woman to another in confusion. "Okay, maybe introductions would be in order here?"

Rachel spared him a quick look before turning back to Angela. "Angel, maybe you'd care to meet Ian Logan."

"Your latest conquest? Not interested." Angel didn't even look at him.

"Logan owns the resort, Angel. He's not...just...my latest conquest." Rachel's amused grin made Logan relax a little.

"Then it was your office that called." Angel gave him a sharp look. "I suppose I should thank you for letting me know where she is."

Rachel's smile froze on her face. "You called her?" She took a step away from him, her eyes shining with betrayal. "Why would you...were you checking up on me?"

Logan sighed. He'd been a magician long enough to know when the jig was up and Rachel's sharp intelligence wouldn't allow for anything but the truth. "I wanted to make sure you were okay. I didn't know, then—"

"It doesn't matter what you didn't know." Her gaze froze him. "You had no right to tell her I was here."

Angel looked strangely satisfied. "So now you can come home."

"Come home?" Rachel snorted. "Right. Have you forgotten there's nothing for me there? What I didn't lose, you took. So no. I won't be going home." She gave Logan another cold glance. "Although I'll be damned if I'll stay here, either. Get out."

Her calm tone frightened him. "Rachel, I didn't mean—"

"Get out." She stalked into the room, plucked up the bottle of Sangria she'd set aside earlier and twisted the cap off. "I've got packing to do."

Logan watched helplessly. He could see the protective sheen forming again. The thaw had been temporary then. She was back to what she wanted to be, no more than a shell of a beautiful woman. He had no idea how to break through to her again. "Rachel, please don't do this."

For answer, she took a long swig from the bottle and wiped her hand across her mouth. "I said get out. Both of you." Still holding the bottle, she stalked away, her head held high, into the bathroom.

"Jesus. You'd better leave." Angel looked around. The door still stood ajar. Logan realized it must not have latched when they came in. Angel raised one eyebrow, looking at him curiously. "What exactly were you guys doing together? You're that magician, aren't you? You really own this place?" She looked around and whistled softly. "Yeah, I guess that's pretty impressive."

"Thank you." He bit the words off sarcastically.

She gave him a look of honest surprise. "I wasn't talking about you."

Damn it. He was really starting to dislike this woman. "And I didn't really mean it, either. And you're leaving too."

"You can't make me leave. She's my sister." She put her hands on her hips belligerently.

"And I own this hotel. Rachel was pretty clear she doesn't want either of us here. If you don't leave, I'll call security." He folded his arms over his chest, glaring at her.

She bit her lip, obviously considering her options. Then she shrugged and walked out. "I'm staying right here, anyway." She motioned toward the room across the hall.

Ignoring her, still angry and worried about Rachel, he turned and started away, not even sure where he was heading.

"I'm taking her home." Her words followed him down the path he hadn't quite chosen yet.

He paused, glancing over his shoulder. "Good luck with that. She didn't seem too certain about going anywhere with you."

"She will. And now she knows you betrayed her—"

"I didn't betray her." He took a deep breath. "I wouldn't do that."

"Doesn't matter." She took a step toward him, her face earnest. "You don't know her. She fucked up—God, so bad. She knows it, I know it, everybody that knows her knows it."

"Whatever she did, she's taking responsibility for it. And I get the feeling maybe you had something to do with the loss of her husband."

Angel's face flushed with combined embarrassment and anger. He smiled as she hurried to cover her momentary discomfiture. "Whatever. She's confused. She doesn't know what's best for her right now."

He looked down at his feet, shoving his hands into his pockets. She was right about that. Maybe he should just let her take Rachel home. Maybe it was the best thing for her. Or maybe it would destroy her. He suspected the latter. He returned his attention to the dark-haired woman and nodded. "At least we agree about something." And he turned away, certain now he had to do something, even if he didn't know what it was.

****

Rachel paced the room, her heart thundering in her chest. How could Logan betray her this way? It didn't matter that he'd been concerned about her. The betrayal hurt all the worse. Calling her sister? Angel? The one person she couldn't see, the one who knew it all. The one person who reminded her what she'd done. Anger warred with anguish, but it was despair that finally won out. She threw herself on the bed, her chest heaving with sobs but the tears refusing to cool her hot cheeks.

She could feel her own heart beating in her chest and she hated it. If it would just stop beating, the pain would finally go away. She hated her sister and Kevin, and even Logan for the brief moment of hope he'd offered her. Before he betrayed her. The darkness inside her chest yawned, and this time she didn't shy away from it.

None of it was worth it. Not the men, not the money, not even the alcohol and the fuzzy nights and painful mornings. She'd always intended it to end, she'd just thought she'd do it slower: death at a snail's pace by sex and alcohol and indiscriminate partying. But that was the coward's way out.

The moment of epiphany stopped the agony of the dry sobs. She rolled over and looked at the ceiling fan, running through the events of the day. For a brief moment in time, she'd thought maybe there was another way, with Logan. But it wasn't even his fault, not really. The need for finality had always been there, at least since the accident.

I should have died then. And she would. Thanks to her sister and Logan, she could find the courage to end it.

Just not here. I won't do it here. The decision felt right. She would leave. Alone. No Logan, no Angel, no sweet Spanish kid who was almost young enough to be her son. And when she got wherever she was going, she'd isolate herself long enough to get it done.

****

Logan stood from behind his desk, rolling his shoulders and staring moodily out the window. This wasn't the way he'd imagined his night. *Damn it.* He turned to the bar, pouring himself a glass of Scotch and taking a sip, enjoying the rich, smoky flavor. If he had a poison, Scotch was it, and he felt the need for it right then. He closed his eyes. *If only her sister hadn't shown up.*

Maybe it's a good thing. Maybe you were too close to betraying Nora. He shook off the thought. No. Nora would want him to help her friend. And he still had a difficult time equating Rachel with the slightly timid young woman who'd been friends with his wife. That certainly wasn't who he'd held in his arms, locked in wanton passion.

Everyone changed. Every experience changed them. Maybe what he'd glimpsed was a bit of the woman who could be. A warm, caring, passionate woman. He wanted to get to know that woman, but he'd been frustrated in his attempt to unlock her.

A light tap on his office door startled him. At this hour, the offices should be deserted. It could only be Tammy, concerned about him as usual. He swore sometimes that she bugged his office. He sighed and prepared himself for her maternal attitude. "Come in."

The door opened and Rachel walked in. She wore a black sundress and she was as stunningly beautiful as the first time he'd seen her. He cleared his throat, trying to sound nonchalant. "To what do I owe this unexpected pleasure?"

"So many things." She took the glass of Scotch from his hand and sniffed it, frowning a little. "What is that?"

"Scotch." He took it back and set it aside. "And not important. What's going on?"

"I want to leave here tomorrow." She dipped her finger in the drink he'd set on the desk, swirled it and then, her eyes on his, put it in her mouth and licked it clean. She smiled a little, moving closer to him.

He forced himself to ignore the rising desire in his chest. He didn't want from her what she was offering...but it was still impossible to tear his eyes from her hypnotic gaze. God, she's beautiful. He dragged his concentration back to the conversation. "You don't need my permission."

"I do need transportation, though."

"Talk to the concierge." He started to turn away. "It's what I pay them for."

She caught his arm. "Don't be that way."

He actually considered giving in. She'd let him make love to her. He was certain of it. But that wasn't what either of them needed. He turned, taking her hand from his arm and holding it between both of his own. "I'll arrange your transportation."

She blinked. "Thank you." She started to turn away, but he held tight. She glanced back at him. "What?"

"Don't leave."

An odd expression flickered over her face at the two words. A simple request for anyone but her, probably. "Why would I stay?" Her lips curved, a cruel imitation of a smile. "Why would you want me to?" She pulled her hand away.

He sat back in his chair, picking up his glass and taking a sip. "I'll have transportation arranged for you by ten o'clock tomorrow."

Island Magic   Michelle Garren Flye

She nodded. "I'll be ready." She started out, but paused, her hand on the doorjamb as if she didn't want to let go yet. She glanced over her shoulder. "For what it's worth, I'm sorry I came here."

The words took his breath away. He knew what she meant by them and it made his heart ache. He sat very still, not trusting himself to speak. The moment she was outside the door, he picked up his phone.

Tony answered on the third ring. "Hey man. You free? We're at the bar. Come on out."

Logan brushed the suggestion aside impatiently. "I need help." He reached for his Rolodex, thumbing through cards furiously. Finding the one he wanted, he pulled it out. "Can you guys come to my office?"

Before Tony could answer, he hung up, dialing the number on the card as fast as he fingers could manage.

He'd save her. Whether she wanted it or not.

Chapter 6

"Are you sure you can do it?" Logan stopped pacing long enough to look at the woman on the computer screen.

"With what you've given me to work with, yeah. The time frame's short, but I've got a crew down there already. It can be done." She pushed her curly mass of blonde hair over her shoulder and leaned forward on the bit of messy desk Logan could see. Her eyes were intent. "Are you sure you want to do it?"

"No." Tony interrupted, turning the computer to face him. "Sabrina, can't you talk him out of this? At best, it's a felony."

"It's not a felony. I'm saving her life." Logan paused in his pacing, looking around the table. Maybe he shouldn't have brought all of them in on this. Technically Tony was right. And by letting them in on his plan, he'd made them all accessories.

Of course, not all of them seemed to mind. Andre, at least, seemed more interested in the mechanics of the trick Logan planned to pull off. He'd brought up several salient points. Even Lydia had gotten into the spirit of it, suggesting a couple of changes in the schedule. And she didn't even like Rachel.

Stacey seemed neutral, though her sharp eyes and ears had obviously taken in everything with a reporter's natural instincts to look and listen. Only Tony had been outspoken in his opposition to the plan. Logan put a hand on his friend's shoulder. "Look, man, if you don't want to be part of this—"

Tony relented and shook his head. "No. If you're doing it, I'm in. I just want you to take a second to think."

Sabrina's teleconferenced voice interrupted over the computer's speaker. "If you want it done, we don't have a second. But Logan, Tony's right. You need to be certain she's worth the risk. You could lose everything with this one." She shrugged. "Or it could turn out to be the greatest trick you've ever pulled off. Just...no one will ever know about it. And I won't lie. It's going to cost you."

Logan brushed the monetary consideration aside with a sweeping motion. "Do it."

Sabrina nodded. "Okay." She sat back, her gentle smile lighting her face briefly. "Nice to see all you guys again."

"You too, Sabrina." As the others echoed his sentiment, Logan reached for the laptop and closed it with a snap. Then he looked around the room again. "Thanks. For being with me on this. I'll take it from here, though." He glanced at Tony. "I'll stay in touch, but less contact is better." He looked at Lydia and Stacey. "You guys will handle the sister, right?"

Lydia made a face of distaste. "If you insist."

"She has to make a clean slate or this isn't going to work at all." Logan leaned on the conference table, palms flat against the smooth wood. He wondered vaguely how much the table cost. Funny how he didn't pay attention to things like that anymore. Sabrina's estimate of the cost of his plan wasn't low, but somehow that cost paled in comparison to the thought of losing her. He could spend millions of dollars on thousands of conference tables—or one magic trick—but the potential loss of one woman left him with a pain in his chest that made it hard to breathe.

Stacey spoke for the first time, her voice gentle. "You love her." At his sharp look and Lydia's frown, she shrugged. "You wouldn't go through all this for just anyone, Logan." She put a hand on her rounded belly. "We don't put ourselves in the way of pain for people we don't care about."

Andre put his hand on top of his wife's and their eyes met for a moment. As if something unspoken passed between them, he nodded. "Well, we should all get some sleep, huh? Tomorrow's going to be busy." He stood, helping her up and turning to Logan. "You'll probably have two, maybe three days. After that, I'm pretty sure we won't be able to stall her sister."

Logan nodded. "I'm supposed to see Jasmine weekend after next." He wondered vaguely if he'd make it. If things didn't go his way, he might be in jail. And how much would that matter to his daughter?

"Tammy will take care of those arrangements. I'll see to it." Tony stood also, his fiancée rising lithely as he did. "And I know you say less contact is better, but I'm checking in daily."

Logan nodded, walking them to the door. As he closed it behind them, he said a quiet prayer. This was the right thing for him to do, the only course of action he could see. If he let Rachel leave tomorrow, he might never see her again. And if his years performing grand illusions had taught him anything, it was that any really good illusion required a good ground team. These guys were some of the best in the business, and with Sabrina's help, he had no doubt they could pull it off. Yes, it was the right thing for him to do. He just hoped bringing his friends in on his plan was the right thing for them.

****

Rachel put the last of her clothes in the suitcase and closed it. She hadn't slept. Instead, she'd spent the evening trying to convince herself she felt no regrets. No doubts. But her eyes kept sliding sideways toward her cell phone. She

106

could call him. Even now she could call him and tell him she'd changed her mind. All it would take would be one call and he wouldn't let her leave. She could stay with him, probably for as long as she wanted. She squelched the tiny, needy voice in her heart that urged her to do just that. Not that she ever would. Not that she even could.

She straightened just as a knock sounded on the door. Thinking it was the bellman, she swung the door open, but it was her sister standing there. Her gaze fell on the suitcase on the bed. "Good. You're packed."

"All packed up and ready to go." Rachel shrugged and moved away from the door. "So you can head home. My fun is over now." She pretended to pout.

"Cut it out, Rachel. Come home and let us help you." Angel shoved her way into the room, as if Rachel were trying to block her.

"Who? You and my pathetic ex-husband?" Rachel snorted.

"Don't!" Angel held up her hands in a stop motion.

"Don't what?" Rachel rounded on her with a snarl. "Don't remind you of your transgressions? Don't point out that you took something that belonged to me? Without asking permission and without waiting until I was done with it? With him, that is."

"We've been over this." Angel looked tired. "Please, Rache, try to understand. You were...so emotionally unavailable at that time and we were all hurting so much. Kevin...he needed someone and so did I, but we never meant for it to happen. God, neither one of us wanted to hurt you that way."

As usual, the explanations did nothing but bore Rachel. She'd heard them all before. Maybe they hadn't meant to hurt her, but they had. Or they would have if there had been anything left of her to hurt by then. Fortunately, perhaps, it was all gone by that point, sucked into the void and leaving only the shell of her former self walking around and going through the motions of living.

Just because it hadn't hurt didn't stop the hate, though. Angel she might have forgiven eventually, but Kevin? The man who, above all others, should have been right there in the void with her? His betrayal was beyond redemption, and her hatred for him was the final push she'd needed to turn her back on all of them.

She reached for the suitcase. "I'm not your problem anymore. Yours or Kevin's. You don't need my permission or my forgiveness. Obviously."

Angel opened her mouth and closed it again. "Where will you go?"

Rachel heaved her suitcase from the bed to the door and fixed her sister with a glare. "I don't need your permission, either. But I'm going to the airport in Cancun. From there? Who knows? I've still got plenty of money to spend. Whatever looks tropical and fun."

"Fun?" Angel snorted. Rachel glanced over her shoulder at her sister. Angel raised her eyebrows. "Really? You expect me to think you're having fun? Drinking yourself into a stupor and sleeping with every man with a pulse?"

"Oh, that's where you're wrong, Sis." Rachel swung around slowly, grinning at the opportunity to taunt her sister. "I'm very selective. Dear God, the men I've been with…" She laughed softly. "Seems I've still got it. I'm not just a trophy wife anymore. I know what it takes to please a man."

"And what about Logan?" Angela took a step toward her sister, her shoulders squared, her attitude as confrontational as Rachel's. Angel always had been able to give back as much as she got.

Like now. "What about him?" Rachel fought to keep her tone even.

"How does he fit into this picture of hedonistic sex? I can't imagine he's the love 'em and leave 'em type you seem to prefer."

Rachel gritted her teeth and forced herself to speak coldly. "Logan doesn't fit into my picture at all. Maybe you'll find he fits with yours. You seem to like picking up my leavings." And she turned, flinging open the door on a startled bellman and stalking past him, preferring to let him figure out the luggage on his own than to continue the conversation with her sister.

****

A limousine took her to the island's little airfield and the driver escorted her to a comfortable waiting room inside the hangar. "Mr. Logan wants you to wait here for your pilot."

Rachel nodded absently. She'd half hoped Logan would appear to say good-bye or even attempt to convince her to stay, but he hadn't. Her whole exit had been so carefully orchestrated, in fact, she couldn't help but believe that he was relieved to see her go. Maybe he'd decided she wasn't worth the effort. And he was right, of course. A man like him could find a woman without all the baggage she carried. A woman who could love him completely with a heart that had never been broken.

Not that it mattered. Millionaire resort owner or local pool boy, he was just another man, and one she couldn't afford to be near. She wanted him, but not like she'd wanted the Spanish kid or any of the other men she'd seduced. She wanted him with a core of her being that wasn't even there anymore. It wasn't possible for her to want anyone this way, let alone Ian Logan. But he'd torn down her defenses and when she rebuilt them, she'd left gaping holes. As if she wanted to let him back in.

Restless, she paced the little waiting room, finding a pot of coffee on a table nearby and deciding to help herself. Just as she started toward it, however, a voice spoke quietly from the door. "I see everything worked out well this morning."

She wheeled to find Logan standing in the door. "Holy God. What are you doing here?" The words were yanked from her in her astonishment and she clapped her lips closed at the end of them, not happy to think they might reveal her pleasure at seeing him.

He smiled, his eyes flickering over her. He looked good in a silky Caribbean blue shirt and light-colored slacks. She glanced down, not surprised to find he wore a pair of raffia flipflop sandals. He moved past her. "You wanted coffee?"

She hesitated, then nodded. He poured a cup. "Cream or sugar?" He glanced at her.

"Black."

He nodded. "I figured." He handed her the cup.

"None for you?" She raised her eyebrows, taking a sip of the scalding liquid and regretting it.

"Never when I fly." At her look of surprise, he shrugged. "Pilots can be hard to come by for unscheduled hops. I'm taking you on my private plane. And I'm the pilot."

She gave him a suspicious look, blowing on the hot coffee before taking another sip. "I hope this isn't some attempt to convince me to stay."

"Oh no. We settled all that last night, didn't we?" He motioned at her mug. "Finish up. It's a short jump to the mainland, but we need to get going. I'm just going to go finish up the pre-flight."

He sounded so chipper she wanted to hit him, but he was out of the room in a moment, and she took another long drink of the cooler coffee, still feeling sluggish and tired. She wished she'd slept more. She sighed and looked around, finally sinking into an armchair. If this cup didn't make her feel more awake, she'd have another. No way was she going to spend her last hour with Logan half asleep.

****

"Rachel!" The voice yanked her into semi-consciousness, or maybe it was the hands gripping her shoulders. God, had she fallen asleep in the waiting room? And why was everything so bright, and why did it all hurt so much? She wanted to tell him to leave her alone, let her rest for a few more minutes, but the anxiety in his voice when he called her name again made her push past the inertia.

"Jesus. What? Did I fall asleep?"

He stared at her for a second, then enfolded her in his arms. "Thank God. For a second I thought..." He stopped, pushing her away from him and she noticed for the first time the black marks on his face.

"God, what happened to you? Were you working on the plane or something?" She pulled away, brushing something gritty from her shoulders, feeling more in her hair. Why was she sandy? She looked around, taking in her surroundings with astonishment. "What?" She returned her gaze to him. "What am I doing on the beach?"

He frowned. "What's the last thing you remember?"

"The waiting room at the airport. What happened? I hurt all over." She struggled to stand, but he stopped her.

"Wait. Take it easy. You don't remember getting on the plane? Maybe you hit your head harder than I thought." He brushed her hair back from her face. "You're not bleeding." His frown deepened. "How do you feel?"

"What do you mean, how do I feel? I feel like a truck ran over me. I told you, I hurt all over." Her voice came out sounding petulant and whiny and she stopped, taking a deep breath. "I'm sorry. I just don't understand. What happened?"

He hesitated, glanced around and finally said, "Let's get out of the sun. It's the middle of the afternoon and you don't have any sunblock on."

She let him help her to her feet, leaning on him as she turned toward the shadier area just off the beach. She stopped, first because she didn't recognize the beach and second because of the smoking, blackened hulk a few hundred feet away. She gasped, her knees buckling beneath her. "Oh my God! Were we on...that?"

"Let's get out of the sun." His voice was very gentle, his arm strong around her. She let herself lean on him, gratitude for his support overwhelming even her shock. He led her to the shade of a palm tree and helped her sit. "Wait here."

Before she could stop him, he went back toward the wreckage, tossing aside some of the lighter pieces, obviously searching for something. She scanned the area. It looked like the set of a Hollywood movie. She felt dizzy and returned her gaze to Logan. His blue silk shirt had torn and blackened in places, but she didn't see any blood. How could they have been in a crash like this one and walked away unharmed?

Relatively unharmed, anyway. She really did feel sore all over. Her head ached and her mouth was dry and she felt more than a little nauseous. Not bad for a woman who'd just escaped a plane crash, though. She might have thought it was a really bad hangover if she didn't know better. She groaned. Way to look at the bright side, Rache.

"Are you all right?" Logan stood beside her, holding a first aid kit.

"Yeah, great. Would you please just tell me what happened?"

He handed her a packet of aspirin and a bottle of water, his expression grim. "What happened is I'm firing whatever mechanic worked on my plane this last time. I told them there was something off with the rudder—"

"Stop!" She tore open the aspirin and swallowed it with a grateful gulp of the water. Had water ever tasted so sweet? She closed her eyes for a minute, then opened them again. "Okay, so there was something wrong with the plane. How did we survive that?"

"We didn't." At her astonished look, he laughed. "I mean we survived; your head wouldn't hurt so bad if we didn't, would it? But most of that happened after I made the emergency landing."

"The emergency landing." Feeling weak, she lay back on the sand. "And you managed that on a beach and dragged us to safety. And I slept through all of it?"

"Like I said, I think you hit your head. But yeah. That's the gist of it." He flopped onto the sand next to her. "If it makes you feel any better, I think I saw some of your luggage had been thrown clear."

"Oh so much better." She turned her head to look at him. Did he actually look cheerful? Was that a little smile in his eyes? "Are you happy about this?"

"Could have been worse." He brushed her hair from her face, his expression sobering. "For a minute there I thought it was worse." His eyes flickered down to her lips and back to meet her gaze. "I like the world better with you in it."

Her lips parted involuntarily and then she sat up, alarm bells clanging in her aching head. "Did you say you saw one of my cases around somewhere? I could use something stronger than aspirin."

He stood with an ease and grace that made her wonder if he could be as sore as she was. "Stay put. I'll bring you what I can find."

For half an hour, he searched the wreckage, bringing her anything he could find that might be useful. Her cosmetic case with the Dramamine and Valium was unfortunately missing, but he easily located the two cases of clothes. When he brought her purse, she had a momentary surge of hope, but it died when she noted the cracked black screen of her cell phone. "So much for that. I don't guess the plane has an emergency beacon, does it?"

"It does. Whether it survived the fire I can't say yet." He studied the still-smoking hulk and cracked open another bottle of water to take a swig. "Probably, but we may have to wait and see." He swiped his arm across his forehead. "Although if I'm right about where we are, at least shelter may not be a problem."

"Really? Why is that?" She tore her eyes away from the open collar of his shirt and the tanned skin beneath. How could a man look so good on a hot day right after they'd both been through a plane crash? Was she actually horny now? What was wrong with her? And how much of her arousal could she blame on survival instinct and how much on the tender look he'd given her? *I like the world better with you in it.*

He seemed not to notice her discomfiture. "Buddy of mine owns a fishing cottage on one of these islands. Not much else here, but he keeps it provisioned and we'll have a roof over our heads." He gave her a measuring look. "Can you walk?"

"Yeah. At least, I think so." She stood, feeling a little unsteady but happy to find her feet would support her. "Yeah. I'm good."

"Great." He picked up her suitcases. "Let's go check it out."

****

Rachel followed him blindly through what seemed like impenetrable jungle. She didn't even care if he was right about the fishing cottage. She just wanted to find a place to lie down and sleep. *Wasn't I just unconscious for who knows how long?* She knew she must be in shock. Who wouldn't be?

And yet as they left the wreck behind on the beach, it felt as if the crash hadn't happened. Except that she was here on some tiny deserted island with Logan when she should be in Cancun planning her next escapade. Her last escapade. And she was actually happy to be alive. "This is so weird."

"Did you say something?" Logan looked over his shoulder. He'd found some sort of knife in the wreckage and had been hacking the undergrowth aside to make a path for them, the heavier of her two bags slung effortlessly over his shoulder. A dark trail of sweat tracked over what was left of his

Caribbean blue shirt. She had a sudden longing to peel that shirt off of him, feel the smooth skin beneath... "Rachel?"

Rachel yanked herself out of her impromptu daydream, hefting the bag she carried into a more comfortable position on her shoulder. "Yeah, sorry. You think your fishing buddy will be here?"

"Doubt it. He's a stock trader, spends most of the year in New York. But every August, like clockwork, he comes down." Logan returned his attention to hacking at vines and palm leaves. "I'm pretty sure he won't mind us using his place though. Considering the circumstances."

"August? Great. Just four months away. I don't suppose he has anything useful like a satellite phone. Or neighbors." Rachel felt the tartness of her words on her tongue and didn't care. She was nearing the point of exhaustion. When was the last time she'd gotten this much exercise? Months. Months of drinking her meals, lounging by the pool—sex had been her only exertion. *Guess it doesn't build up this kind of stamina.* She smiled to herself, but then her ankle turned under her and she stumbled.

He caught her with the non-knife wielding arm. "You okay?"

She shook her head. "I think I'm really far from okay, actually."

"Well, hang in there. If I'm right about where we are, we're almost there." Still supporting her with one arm, he cut aside the underbrush with several more swipes and they emerged into a clearing.

At first, she almost didn't realize that the clearing was actually more of a lawn. Not exactly a neatly kept lawn, but grass, nonetheless, with only a couple of palm trees and some shrubs and...

"I guess I was right about where we are." Logan released her as she stared in wonder at the house in front of them.

By fishing hut standards, it was pretty damn nice. It blended in with its surroundings, the gray-green shingles of the walls mimicking the palm trees. The brownie-yellow roof at first looked like thatch, but she realized it was another impersonation of the natural surroundings. The jungle equivalent of a modern log cabin. A stone walkway led up to the front door, where Logan was even then looking for a key under the mat. He produced it with triumph. "Ta da. We don't even have to break a window."

She hurried to stand beside him, clutching his hand in hers, suddenly unwilling to be alone. Her body shuddered, which was ridiculous in the sweltering ninety-degree heat of the jungle. He paused, his arm going around her, his expression concerned. "Are you okay? You're shivering."

"I'm—" Fine. The word was on her tongue, and she choked on it, and she could only shake her head, feeling weak and tired and—for once—not afraid to let him know that. And the horrible shuddering continued, as if she were in an arctic landscape and not the Central American jungle. She shook until her teeth rattled. She turned her eyes imploringly to him. What's wrong with me?

"You're in shock." He put both arms around her, massaging her and holding her close. "Jesus. I can't believe I didn't think of that. You've been through so much." The gentle way he spoke and the loving way he held her warmed her a little, helping her relax into his arms.

He ushered her inside, but she didn't look around, her vision dimming so she could only concentrate on what was immediately in front of her. He helped her to a soft surface and she collapsed, feeling him cover her with a blanket. He disappeared for a moment, and panic threatened to eclipse what little was left of her sense. She sat up. "Logan!"

"It's okay, baby." And it was. He was there with more blankets than she would have thought existed in the jungle. He covered her with them, then lay down beside her, holding her, stroking her hair, somehow managing to ease the horrible tension that held her in its grip.

As she relaxed, she closed her eyes, but then she opened them again. "Don't leave me."

He smiled into her eyes, brushing her hair back from her face. "There's nothing on God's earth I'd rather do than fall asleep with you in my arms, sweetheart."

His words warmed her from the inside, and she sat up, pushing the blankets away, then lay back in his arms. A tiny shiver ran through her and his arms tightened protectively, as if by instinct. Feeling safer than she ever had before, she buried her face in his torn shirt.

Chapter 7

It was darker when she woke, and he was gone. One of the blankets covered her, and she sat up, feeling completely rested and surprised to find the pain was gone. She stretched and looked around. The light looked different, like late afternoon, almost evening. She must have been asleep for a couple of hours.

The interior of the little cabin was as surprising as the exterior. Marble floor stretched from one end of the large room to the other, and extravagant jungle scenes adorned all the walls except one, which was one large window. A half partition with a granite countertop divided a small kitchen area from the living/dining room. A door opened off to the left, probably to a bedroom. The furnishings were plain but sumptuous. The couch she'd slept on was made of some microfiber material softer and more luxurious than anything else she'd ever experienced.

"This is a fishing cottage?" She spoke out loud without meaning to. A second later, Logan came out of the bedroom.

"You're awake." He smiled. "Thank God. Are you all right? Do you feel okay? Any disorientation?"

She stretched again. "I'm fine. In fact, I feel great. Those must have been some pretty good aspirin."

Something flickered in his eyes. Relief? But before she could question it, he stood briskly. "Well, if we're going to be stranded on an island, this is the way to do it. While you were out, I turned on the hot water. The place is run on a generator and a geothermal HVAC. It'll take a while before things get going, but once it does, we'll have almost all the comforts of home."

He walked into the kitchenette and rummaged through the cabinets. "Not bad. A lot of canned and dried stuff. Some spices. Ahh." He turned, holding a bottle in his hand. "Yet another thing Jake and I agree on."

She raised her eyebrows. "Whisky?"

He tsked. "For a drinker, you don't know much about alcohol, do you?"

"Not really." She rubbed her aching feet, glad he'd taken off her sandals. Why, oh why hadn't she worn flipflops or tennis shoes or those cute little hiking boots she'd noticed in the boutique window the other day? Of course, to be fair, she hadn't counted on hiking through a jungle today. But that didn't help her sore feet much. "I only ever drank wine before—" She paused, frowning. She'd almost said "before the accident," and she didn't want to make a confession now. As soon as they were rescued she would be nothing but a memory to him.

"Scotch." He held the bottle closer to her, as if it would make a difference. "The Macallan 1926, to be exact. It's sixty years old and it costs $54,000…on a bad day."

"Okay." She nodded. "Quite a discovery. We'll have a party later."

"You don't party with Scotch. It's too civilized a drink. You sip and appreciate. There's a whole art to it." He frowned. "I think Jake's got some Glenlivet in there, too. We'll start there. You'll need to perfect your skills before I'm willing to risk his fury by letting you at his Macallan."

She raised her eyebrows. "At the moment, I'm more interested in a shower. Didn't you say something about hot water?"

"Yeah, but it'll take a while." He set the bottle aside and came over to her, squatting down in front of her and taking her hands in his, his fingers on the inside of her wrists. His expression was concerned. "You look tired again. Why don't you lie down for a while and I'll let you know when the shower's good and warm?"

He was right. She was tired. Again. Wondering when that had happened, she nodded and lay back on the couch, feeling him cover her with an afghan as her consciousness grayed out.

****

Logan spotted Tony pacing the dock as he came over the last dune. He looked anxious, and he didn't wait for Logan to get to him. He nearly ran down the dock, calling, "Is she okay?"

"Still groggy, and in and out of consciousness, but we expected that. And she bought it. All of it. Jeez, Sabrina did a fantastic job. That old plane wreck was very convincing." Logan grinned, feeling the rush he always felt with a successful act. He'd almost forgotten this feeling of triumph.

"Jesus, Logan. Get a grip, man. You just drugged and kidnapped a woman and you're acting like it's the greatest illusion you ever pulled off." Tony glared at his friend. "You're certain she's okay?"

His friend's worried tone got Logan's attention, and he gripped Tony's arm. "It's okay. Her vitals are fine, so don't worry." He scanned the parcels they'd unloaded from the boat earlier when they came to the island. "I should be able to get most of these in one load. I'll store the rest in the shed. I don't have much time, though. I don't know how long she'll sleep."

"You got what I said about kidnapping, right?" Tony folded his arms over his chest.

Logan stacked the parcels he would need immediately in one pile and began hoisting the others to take to the storage shed at the end of the dock. It was waterproof and sealed against the moist heat, so everything would be fine there, and he should be able to come back for supplies on a regular basis, even if he had to wait until she was asleep.

"Are you listening?" Tony shook his head and picked up a stack of boxes to carry to the shed. "I can't believe I let you talk me into this. More than that I can't believe you pulled it off."

"Amazing what money, manpower and a little know-how can do, isn't it?" Logan shot his friend a look. "I never thought I'd need those Hollywood skills again, but they did come in handy today. Come on, man. You can't tell me you aren't feeling a little high off this one, too."

Tony opened his mouth as if to protest, then shrugged. "Okay, yeah. But this is serious, and we've got to be ready to deal with the consequences. You've kidnapped that woman and I'm an accessory."

"It's not going to come to that." Logan tried to sound soothing. Second thoughts couldn't get in his way now. Not now that he was on the right track to saving Rachel. He stacked his own boxes and Tony's neatly into the shed and looked back down the dock. How many times had he watched the sunset from here? And what had he been thinking on those solitary evenings? That he'd like someone to share it with. "Look, it's going to be okay. I'm so close to getting through to her. And she was on a self-destructive path before. I honestly believe she would have committed suicide if I hadn't interfered. She still will if I take her back too soon. I can't really make things worse for her." He paused. "Did her sister buy that I took her to Cancun?"

Tony made a dismissive gesture. "Stacey handled her. She's good with that kind of thing. Has her convinced that you took Rachel off on some romantic getaway." He snorted. "Although why you'd need to leave the island for that, I don't know." He gave Logan a sharp look. "You know she's really worried about her sister, right?"

"She should be." Logan felt his features twist a little with distaste. He shook it off. Angela didn't matter now. He couldn't afford to spend time on negative emotions. He needed to concentrate on Rachel and convincing her that healing was what she really wanted. "I just need a couple of days. Maybe a week, I don't know. I just need to convince her she can believe again."

"Believe in what?" Tony spread his hands. "Magic? Life? What is it that you want this woman to believe in, Logan? You?"

He shook his head. "Something much more elemental and necessary." He gazed at the sunset for a moment before turning back to his friend. "Love."

****

Rachel woke to the smell of sizzling meat and rolled over on the soft bed. Disoriented, she sat up, gazing out the picture window at the twilit jungle and the memory came rushing back to her of the airplane crash. God, was that all for real? She stretched, relieved the achiness hadn't returned. She still felt sweaty and grimy, though. A moment later, she wondered how she'd gotten to the bedroom. Logan must have moved her so she'd be more comfortable.

She heard whistling from the kitchen and stood, poking her head out the door. Logan stood by the stove, browning something heavenly smelling in a pan. He'd obviously showered and now wore a new pair of jeans and a t-shirt with the logo of a pub in London. He looked natural in these surroundings, as if he belonged there. When he glanced up a lock of his black hair fell over his eyes.

"Hey, sleepyhead. Feeling better?" In spite of his light tone, she sensed a touch of worry.

Her heart gave a little extra thumpety-thump before she managed to settle it into a regular rhythm. She yawned, covering her mouth. "Yeah, much. What are you making?"

"Best damn pasta you'll ever taste. Pancetta with mozzarella-olive sauce. You'll love it." He grinned. "Hope you're hungry."

"I am, actually." As if in agreement, her stomach growled and she laughed. "Where did you find pancetta?"

"Jake has a deep freeze. He keeps meat like pancetta and ham there all year. Even a couple steaks, although it'll probably take a day or two to defrost them." He appeared unworried. "The water's plenty warm now if you want to shower."

"Great." She tilted her head, studying him. "Good thing your buddy Jake is always prepared. Was he a boy scout or something?"

He laughed. "Doubt it. Not really his thing. But he does like to live well, even when he's down here."

"I'll say." She snorted. "I know my brains were sort of scrambled by the crash, but do I remember you showing me a fifty thousand dollar bottle of whisky?"

"Scotch." He drained the now crispy pancetta without removing it from the pan and turned. "And yes, but we won't break into that one unless we get desperate. I want to make sure I can replace anything we use and I can't swear I can find another one of those."

"Unless we get desperate? How long do you figure we're going to be here, anyway?" She couldn't disguise her dismay. "Not that this is a bad place to be stranded. As deserted islands go, it's pretty awesome. Hot tub, fire pit, stocked pantry, Scotch..." She shrugged. "But still. We've got lives, right? I mean, you've got a life to live and I've got one to fritter away."

He set the pan on the stovetop and took a step closer to her. He brushed the back of his hand across her face and bent to kiss her gently on the lips. The caress lasted only an instant, but by the time he drew away, she felt as if she might not mind spending a few days here with him. Alone. With a soft bed and food and drink and no one arriving from the life she'd once lived to remind her of all she'd done wrong. Here she might at last be able to let it all go.

For that instant, she felt as if she teetered on the brink of something powerful enough to shrink the yawning black abyss so it couldn't swallow her.

Heaven. She raised her eyes to his, knowing he could read her heart there. She wanted to lean into him and stay there, and at the moment she didn't care if he knew. *Oh Nora, how could you leave this man?* The thought brought her to her senses at the memory of what would have been if their flight had been uninterrupted. *I was going to go somewhere and end it all. I was going to leave him forever, too.*

She stepped back, shaking her head. "Sorry. I'm still disoriented. I—I need a shower. And food." She turned, determined to get away from him. "I stink. I'll...be right back." She glanced over her shoulder, wondering if he could see her escape for what it was, but he just turned back to the stove without another word. She felt a rush of regret that she quickly diverted and dammed up in a corner of her heart. She couldn't afford to regret. Not that, anyway. What she ought to regret was the fact that he might die with her on this island.

But they weren't going to die. In spite of the plane crash—crash landing, she reminded herself—and the thick jungle surrounding them, she felt strangely safe. The sensation was like an old garment she'd discovered in the back of her closet and put on to find it still fit perfectly...but she didn't like the color anymore.

I don't want to be safe. I want to die so I won't hurt anymore.

A shower was exactly what she needed. She let the hard, hot water pummel her skin, lathered with the soap he'd left and stepped out of the shower feeling new. She towel-dried her dark hair and put on a red sundress, painting her lips with the same shade of lipstick. She studied her image in the mirror. She looked sexy and untouchable and desirable all at the same time. An apt reflection of the turmoil of emotions she couldn't avoid and wasn't sure how to suppress much longer.

****

Logan set the table on the terrace, resolutely focusing on the task at hand and not the beautiful woman in his shower. When the food was on the table and she hadn't emerged, he sank onto the outdoor couch facing onto the jungle, listening to the scratchy sounds of the insects and the far-off calls of birds and other animals. He smiled a little at the illusion of isolation he'd created here. He'd done it for himself originally, a compromise between his desire to keep the island totally natural and still share it with others. On this tiny island he could feel totally alone.

And yet, it was in actuality only a few miles away from Isla Foriscura. At the right point on the island you could see its bigger sister, easily reachable by boat. Everything on the island was the way he'd found it except for the dock, the little cottage and the beach he'd loaned to Sabrina a few years ago to stage a plane crash for a movie. The same one he'd used today for his magic trick.

The magic trick with an audience of one. Rachel. A woman he admired, a woman in pain, a woman who needed real magic in her life. And though he hoped she'd find it here, he still felt a little guilt for fooling her. What would Nora think of him bringing her friend here under false pretenses? What would Nora think of the way he'd begun to feel about Rachel? He shook off the doubts, forcing himself to clear his head of all but the sounds of the jungle.

He'd named the tiny bit of land "Foriscurita", which suited it well. It was his tiny outdoor cure, his escape from the busy resort, which was both more and less than what he'd planned. Foriscurita, in spite of its small size, was home to hundreds of animals, thousands of insects. He heard the faint but distinct muffled growl of a howler monkey and smiled. The first time he'd heard that sound, he'd been certain it was a tiger, even though he knew it was impossible. He'd been fascinated when his guide told him about the howler monkey, who could be heard up to five kilometers away and whose call was only slightly less noisy than a train.

He closed his eyes, listening to the jungle song, feeling, as he had from the first moment he set foot on the island, that it was full of magic. A much more elemental magic than what he'd performed on the Strip of Las Vegas or on Broadway in New York. And much, much more true than what he'd let himself be twisted into when he went to Hollywood.

The howler monkey's call echoed through the jungle and into his heart.

"Dear God, what was that?" Rachel's voice sounded startled.

He opened his eyes and turned to her, at peace again with himself. Stronger than he had been. "Howler monkey. No worries. He's probably harmless and certainly miles away."

"Miles away?" She cocked her eyebrow dubiously. "He didn't sound like he was miles away."

He stood. "Trust me. If he were any closer, you'd know." He moved to the table and uncovered the dishes. "This should be hot, if you're hungry."

She stepped away from the door and he noticed the red sundress that hugged her curves just right. His gaze swept over her, appreciating her beauty in the same way he'd enjoy a beautiful piece of art. But when he caught sight of her bare feet, he frowned. "Jesus."

She glanced down. "That's just what happens to feet when you hike two miles through thick jungle in high heels. Nothing to worry about."

"They look bruised." He peered closer. "Are you sure you're all right?"

"I'll be fine. As soon as I drink my wine. More of your friend Jake's private reserve?" She placed her napkin in her lap, picking up the glass and studying the chardonnay with interest, passing it under her nose to catch a whiff of the scent. "God, that smells wonderful." She took a deep sip and set it aside.

He considered her with interest. A friend had once told him what he'd always considered a basic truth about alcoholics: If you think someone has a problem with alcohol, you're probably right. He'd always agreed with this assessment. For the most part, he figured most people probably did have some basic problem with alcohol. Not many people could resist the euphoric influence of fermented beverages—that feeling that nothing could go wrong, nothing ever had gone wrong, and even if something did go wrong, you wouldn't really care. Most of his guests arrived half toasted and spent the rest of their stay working on staying that way.

Yet here sat a woman who he'd been certain was an alcoholic and possibly had a drug problem, too, calmly sipping her wine and setting it aside to concentrate on her food. Maybe alcohol isn't her addiction at all. The thought was unsettling considering what he knew about her sex life. He'd heard of sex addicts. But he didn't think that was Rachel, either. Which brought him back to whatever the trauma was she'd suffered. Her husband's desertion didn't fully account for it. It was as if she'd lost everything and when she put it back together, it was crooked.

She looked up from her plate. "Aren't you eating?"

"Yeah." He picked up his knife and fork. "What do you think?"

She took a bite. "It's very good. I'm actually having a hard time convincing myself I'm on a deserted island."

He smiled. "Yeah. I guess so."

"Lucky for us we crash-landed on your friend's beach, huh?" She smiled, her sharp intelligence shining through her gaze and making him wonder if she'd already caught onto him.

"Maybe it wasn't luck." He met her gaze. "Maybe it was fate."

"You believe in fate?" She raised her eyebrows.

He pushed his plate away and picked up his wine, studying the golden liquid, playing for time. "You know about Nora. I told you everything."

"You don't believe that was fate." The shock in her voice rang through the night noises of the jungle.

"I believe in some instances you make your own fate. Or choose it." He set the wine aside and leaned over the table, peering into her eyes. "I believe in fate in as far as I believe we are fated to reach certain points in our lives where we have to make decisions. But I believe the decisions we make are our own."

She looked away, running one finger over the rim of her glass. "You believe I'm making the wrong choices, then, choosing the wrong fate. Like Nora."

He shook his head. "I only know how I feel about my own choices. But I don't want to see you destroy yourself."

"Like Nora." Her direct gaze challenged him. Tell me I'm wrong.

"I didn't say that." He refused to turn away. "But yes. That's the path you're on, isn't it?"

She stood, taking her glass with her. For a long moment, she stood on the edge of the patio, her bare feet just barely not touching the grass. The full moon turned the jungle into a mass of curving, blue and black shadows. He could see her stance slowly relax and she took the last sip of the wine, setting the glass aside and turning back to him. "This place is amazing." She laughed. "I'm almost glad we crashed here."

"Well, if we had to crash, this is the place to do it." He shrugged. It was better not to push too hard. He'd let her change the subject.

She moved over to the edge of the hot tub and peered in. He'd uncovered and started it earlier, more for atmosphere than anything, but it occurred to him it might be what her feet needed. He moved to a chair close by. "It's okay." He indicated the tub. "I cleaned it and checked it earlier. It's safe. No snakes."

"Snakes?" She didn't appear concerned, her voice almost absent. "That's good." She sat, dangling her feet in the warm water and closing her eyes in unfeigned pleasure. "Oh, that's nice."

She might have been on vacation. Just any woman on vacation in a Central American jungle after a plane crash. The absurdity of it made him wince, bringing back a little of his earlier guilt.

As if reading his mind, she opened her eyes. "Aren't you worried?"

"About being rescued? Not really. We can survive pretty comfortably here for weeks. And they'll be looking for us by now."

She closed her eyes again. "I wish they wouldn't. I could stay here. I might even be happy…after a while." She smiled a little. "Don't you ever wish for that? Just sweet oblivion and no one to bother you."

Yes. "I'm here. Won't I bother you?" To prove his point, he moved behind her, massaging her shoulders. She felt tense, but not as bad as she might have after all she'd been through.

"Umm." She stretched like a cat, rolling her head back so she looked up at him. "I doubt it. At least, not in the way you mean."

He smiled a little and stepped away. "In the mood to try something new?"

"You mean the Scotch or something better?"

"Let's start with the Scotch." He retreated to the kitchen, ready to regroup. She'd sounded so lost when she spoke about her wish to stay on the island. He couldn't help but wonder what would happen when she found out he'd lied about the crash. Or misled her, anyway. He rummaged the cupboard, finding the bottle and glasses and deciding it didn't really matter one way or the other. What was done, was done.

She'd removed her bruised feet from the hot tub, but she still sat on the edge, looking like a girl with her knees drawn up to her chin as she looked out at the jungle. He paused, trying to remember what it was like to really experience the jungle for the first time, and she turned her luminous eyes on him. "Oh good. Drinks."

"Not just drinks." He shook his head reprovingly, handing one glass to her as he took a seat a safe distance away on the sofa. "Scotch. This is The Glenlivet 15 French Oak Reserve."

"Oh, The Glenlivet? Not just any Glenlivet, then?" Her eyes sparkled with amusement and he felt an answering smile on his own lips. He couldn't help it. She affected him that way.

He tsked. "Now, now, don't take this lightly. It's serious." Only when she assumed a deliberate solemn face did he continue, swirling the reddish-amber liquid in his glass. "The first thing you'll notice about the taste is the burned flavor. Enjoy it. Savor it. It'll never be like that again."

She laughed out loud. "Really? Jeez, this is serious. I feel like I'm losing my virginity all over again."

"Really. It's surprising, if you think about it, how many things truly aren't the same the second time around. It might be better, but it'll never be the same as the first time." Like the jungle. Like sex. Like love... He took a sip of his drink, the ice cubes clinking a little. His eyes met hers and he smiled a little at the consternation he saw there. "Go ahead."

"Are you going to watch?" She raised her glass to her lips, letting it hover there. God, how could she make drinking sexy? Was there anything about this woman he didn't find attractive, though? Even earlier when he'd glimpsed the hurt little girl inside the sexy woman...even then he'd wanted her. God help him.

He cleared his throat and took another sip of his drink, barely noting the taste. He liked Glenlivet. It was nothing compared to the Macallan, of course, but she was hardly ready for that. He held the woody flavored liquor in his mouth for a moment before letting it trickle down his throat. Finding his resolve again, he looked back at Rachel. Only then did she take her first sip of the drink.

Did she intentionally make everything she did sensual, or was it a total accident? He couldn't be certain, but he suspected the latter. Still, she knew how to play her natural sensuality to her favor, and she did it mercilessly. She savored the drink for a moment, then dropped onto the couch beside him. He couldn't take his eyes off her mouth, and when she dipped her finger in the Scotch and smoothed some over her lips, he accepted the invitation without question, leaning forward to taste her, unsure if it was the scotch or her that gave him the heady sensation.

Only when she moved onto his lap, straddling him, her skirt hiking dangerously up her thighs and her still damp feet pressing against his legs did he come to his senses. "No. We can't do this."

"I beg to differ." She chuckled, rocking her hips against him. "God, you're so hard."

He was. He could feel the blood pulsing in all the wrong spots. He couldn't take advantage of her now, though. It would be tantamount to rape, considering he'd kidnapped her to get her here. And his reasons for kidnapping her did not include having sex with her. At least not like this.

But how on earth was he supposed to find the strength to resist her?

"It would feel so good, wouldn't it?" She whispered the words against his ear and began to kiss his neck, her hands moving beneath his t-shirt. "I've always heard sex after a traumatic experience is amazing."

She was good at the whole seduction game. The realization perversely gave him the strength to do what he had to do. Placing his hands on her waist, he stood, turning her over so she sat on the couch with him straddling her.

She smiled up at him. "Oh, baby. Works for me." But her eyes flickered with doubt. She wasn't used to men taking the initiative, and it hadn't been in her plans for tonight, either. She wanted to maintain control.

He smiled back at her. "We're not doing this."

"Could've fooled me." She slipped her hand beneath the waistband of his jeans and he moved away quickly.

He rolled over on his back, his heart beating faster than he liked. "You've been through enough today."

"Really?" She sat up and crossed her legs, giving him a very reasonable look. "What am I, a delicate flower? I'm willing, you're willing, at least from the feel of you." Her lips curved.

"Let's just do it. Relieve the tension. Call it survival sex or something."

For half a second he teetered on the brink of giving in to her, but it wouldn't be right. Not tonight. She was emotionally damaged, and until she accepted the fact that she could heal, he needed to resist his all too natural impulses.

He stood. "You take the bed. I'll sleep on the couch."

She groaned, leaning her head back on the cushions. "You're really no fun at all, you know?" She reached for the Scotch. "Besides, I didn't finish my drink, and I doubt you want that to go to waste."

He shook his head, a little smile twisting his lips in spite of himself. "Go ahead and finish your drink. I'll get ready for bed."

"Fine." She took a sip. "If you change your mind, you know where I am. And the bed is big enough for two."

He waved over his shoulder as he retreated, trying not to feel like the coward he was starting to think he was.

****

Rachel woke, sweating, from the nightmare. A shriek split the night outside and she clutched the blankets closer, wondering if she'd actually heard the sound or if it had been left over from her nightmare. Hadn't it been the squeal of brakes instead of something jungle-related? She lay flat on her back, disoriented, the sheets tangled around her.

How long had it been since she'd had the dream? The horror of it clung to her like spider webs. For months she'd managed to smother it with alcohol and drugs, but tonight it had come back in force. She bit her lip against the wave of anger and terror and sorrow, but above all the other useless emotions rose self-loathing. Oh God, how had she let it happen? She almost welcomed the dark pit that opened in her middle. If only she could throw herself into it and disappear instead of reliving the all-too clear memory of the afternoon everything changed.

...the heavy traffic...the piercing sun...her head ached...she reached for the visor...

The rest of the memory was a blur. Rachel remembered the sharp, hard shot of terror followed by a lot of screaming and pain and blackness. She groaned, covering her face. She couldn't escape. She couldn't disappear. Her punishment was to smother in her own hatred of herself, alternately trying to hide in a haze of alcohol or lose herself in sexual pleasure. But no matter what she did, in the end she couldn't escape the pain of loss. Tears wouldn't come anymore. She'd cried herself dry, and no matter how much she cried, she couldn't get away from the knowledge that what she'd lost had been her own fault. She sat up, hugging her knees to her chest, wishing for more wine, more Scotch...God, if only they'd found her cosmetic case with the Valium.

"Rachel?" She felt his weight on the bed, his hand on the back of her head. "Sweetheart, are you all right?"

The tenderness of his voice soothed her self-loathing. When he scooped her into his arms and held her against him, she let herself lean her head against his chest, feeling his heart beat and knowing this was a good man who held her. A good man who was doing his damnedest to remain good in spite of...her.

Damnit. She wanted to wail and cry and hit him. She wanted him to stop resisting her, but not so she could drown herself in him temporarily. She wanted him to make love to her...to offer her the solace and peace she'd never sought before even though she needed them desperately. Her own thoughts were like freezing ice water in her spine, propelling her out of his arms and off the bed, not stopping until her back was against the wall.

He looked puzzled. "Rachel? Are you all right?"

She nodded, feeling numb, welcoming the numbness because it hid the other emotions she couldn't stand to feel right then. "I—a nightmare. That's all. Sorry."

"Can I do anything for you?" He stood slowly, as if she were a stray kitten he didn't want to frighten.

Oh, so much. She shook her head, not trusting her voice.

"Okay." He nodded acceptance. "Come back to bed?"

Jesus. If he only knew what those words, spoken so gently, did to her. She took a half step away from the wall and stopped. She couldn't go any closer. If she did, she wouldn't be able to resist the knowledge that in his arms, finally, she could find the relief she knew she didn't deserve. As if he understood, he nodded again and started to the door, pausing with his hand on the knob. "I'll be right outside—if you need anything."

Again, she didn't trust her voice. She slid beneath the sheets, suddenly wishing she'd put on something besides the silk nightie that barely fell to mid-thigh. Dear God, and he'd held her in his arms. Of course, she had put the nightie on in the hopes that he'd see her in it, but her viewpoint had been totally different then. At that time, she'd thought all she wanted from him was sex. Now she knew something different was at stake. She closed her eyes, letting herself admit what she'd kept at bay since the moment she'd first seen him. It wasn't his body she wanted. It wasn't sex she wanted. At least, not just those things.

My God, I want him to be in love with me, but I can't allow that to happen.

Chapter 8

Rachel woke to the sounds of the jungle the next morning with a definitive feeling of unreality. An absolute certainty that the ground under her feet would shift if she took a step. And she knew it all came from her middle of the night reality check. She couldn't be in love. She didn't deserve love. Especially not from a man like Logan. Hell, she hadn't even deserved Kevin's love, a fact he'd made very clear. She winced in a pain that hadn't moved from immediate to remembered.

And that's not even the half of it. The blackness in her heart sat up and yawned, more than ready to wake with her. She clutched it to her, welcomed it to her soul like a lover into her body. *If he knew what a selfish coward I was, he'd hate me just as much as Kevin did.*

"Jesus, Rachel, what the hell do you expect me to feel? If you hadn't panicked..."

Rachel threw back the covers, reaching for her luggage at the same time. She needed more clothes. She couldn't face Logan dressed like this. Not after last night's insight into her own heart. Lust was one thing. She could spend the rest of her life on lust. It was a shield that didn't involve anything important. Lust protected her.

But love, oh God, love was different. Love exposed her, laid her naked and yearning under the bright jungle sun. She needed clothes to hide her heart, and she found them beneath all the bikinis and sundresses. A pair of jeans and a heather-grey cotton t-shirt. The t-shirt wasn't as loose-fitting as she would have liked, but at least it wasn't overtly attractive.

Still feeling vulnerable, Rachel crept from the bedroom to find the kitchen and living room empty. The afghan was neatly folded over one arm of the couch, the pillow he'd borrowed from the bed laid across it. His shoes were by the door leading out onto the patio from the kitchen. She followed her nose to the heavenly aroma of coffee and found a pot brewing in the Cuisinart coffeemaker. Good Lord, is there nothing this place is not equipped with? This Jake guy really likes living well.

She poured herself a cup of the lava-like liquid and went to stand by the window, wondering where Logan had gone, imagining him off searching the jungle for supplies or help. Movement caught her peripheral vision.

Logan stood at the other end of the cleared area around the house, his body moving in the slow, rhythmic way of Tai Chi. He wore light-colored, loose-fitting pants and his chest was bare. His expression was one of deep concentration. Even at a distance, he was god-like in his appearance.

He was far enough away so she wouldn't disturb him if she opened the door. She bit her lip, still hesitant, and watched him for another moment. A bead of sweat trickled down one pectoral muscle. She imagined licking it off, and smiled at the thought. Absurdly reassured by the lust—how could she be falling in love with him if she could imagine using his body the way she did?—she opened the door and stepped outside.

The tropical sun pressed down and she stepped back into the shade cast by the eaves, sipping her coffee and watching the way his muscles lengthened and contracted in the movements of the exercise. He made it look easy, but she'd done a couple of classes of Tai Chi a few years ago. It wasn't easy. It was harder than the yoga class she'd taken up after, and that had been damn hard.

Of course, that was another life, when it had been more important to stay in shape, to keep her weight down, to be the perfect wife. That part of her was gone now. She could stand here on the patio of the fishing cottage in the middle of a Central American jungle and watch a sexy, six-foot-six ex-magician and think about all the things she'd like to do with him in the tangled sheets of the bed she'd just left and not even feel it was anything out of the ordinary.

The longer she watched, however, the less important his body became. It was as if she could see the spirit of the man moving above the physique she already admired. He moved in concert with the jungle's noises, or maybe the jungle had learned his routine and sang him through it. At any rate, as she watched him, she felt a strange peace settle over her soul, along with a longing to keep it that way. She wanted to feel this way forever.

He finished his workout with a final stretching move, then placed both hands at his sides and executed a little bow eastward, as if to the sun. The harmony in the air and in her heart dissipated, so when he turned toward the house, she stepped out of the shade and pretended to applaud. "That was...well done." She let more carnal feelings overwhelm the mental calm she'd achieved while watching him and smiled as her eyes swept over him. "Very nice."

"Thank you." He appeared undisturbed by her lascivious looks as he strode toward the house. "Did you sleep well?"

No mention of the middle of the night. She swallowed her gratitude. "Yes. Sort of. Is it always this noisy here?"

He laughed, looking around at the jungle that buzzed and hummed with life. "Yeah. Pretty much. Except when it rains. But then it's just a different kind of noise."

"Great." She sighed. "It'll take some getting used to."

"Well, maybe we won't be here long enough for you to get used to it." He glanced at the sky. "Could be any time now. Keep an eye out for the rescue choppers."

She spared the sky only a quick glance, knowing she didn't want to see anything there. Rescue meant a return to reality and that wasn't what she wanted at all. She shook off the creeping dread and realized how hot she was. Jeans might not have been her best wardrobe choice after all. "Well, if we're stuck here for the time being, we should make the most of it. What do you do for fun out here?"

"Me?" He opened the glass door and stood back to let her enter first. She welcomed the cooler air and leaned on the counter to watch as he grabbed a towel from the back of a chair and scrubbed his arms and face before looping it over his shoulders. He turned back to her. "Not that I've spent that much time here, but there's always the beach. And I did go on a few hikes with Jake. There are some pretty spectacular views."

"And fishing holes, I guess."

At his startled look, she shrugged. "You said your friend was a fisherman, right? Or that this was his fishing cottage?" She frowned at his reaction.

"He is." Logan looked thoughtful, then turned to the stove. "Surf fishing, mostly. Let's eat and then I'll show you some stuff."

"Stuff?" She raised her eyebrows. "And what are we gonna eat?"

"I'm thinking pancakes." He rummaged in the cupboard and produced a large box of pancake mix and a bottle of syrup.

"Mmm. Is there anything your Jake didn't think of?" She sighed. "Okay. But if we're going to look at 'stuff', what should I wear?"

"What you've got on is good for hiking through the jungle." He tossed her a grin as he turned back to the stove. "Better shoes than yesterday, though. And you might want to bring a swimsuit. We'll take a break and a swim this afternoon."

She turned to the bedroom. Had she even packed any tennis shoes? And if she hadn't, could he magically produce some? It seemed right then that nothing was beyond his power.

****

An hour later with what she had to admit were some delicious pancakes filling her belly, Rachel followed Logan willingly into the jungle, trusting his reassurances that it wasn't far. She still wished she'd bought the hiking boots she'd noticed at the boutique, but her Keds were definitely better suited to the terrain than the high-heeled sandals of the day before.

I might just toss those. When we get back to civilization. If we get back to civilization. She frowned at the thought, then shrugged it off. She'd never exactly counted on being plane-wrecked, but, hey. What the hell? If life handed you lemons... She scanned the attractive, muscular back of the man in front of her. That's some damn good-looking lemonade. The trail they followed was at least an actual trail, not a hacked out path through the jungle, but it was narrow in places and he went ahead of her in those spots, holding back the branches and vines that had encroached on the path.

Yes, if she was going to be plane-wrecked on a deserted island, at least it was with a man like Logan. And on an island he obviously knew his way around. And it actually felt good to be dressed in jeans again and not worrying about reapplying her makeup. She smiled a little as a trickle of sweat cooled a path from her hairline to her chin. Damn if the physical exertion wasn't actually invigorating, too. Exhausting after so many weeks of avoiding it, though. She was very glad when he pulled aside a last set of vines and they stepped out onto a stretch of beach.

It wasn't the beach she'd awakened on after the plane crash. This one looked like something off a postcard. She stepped out onto the white sand, looking around in wonder at the palm trees arching toward the calm, blue Caribbean Sea. Sandy jetties curved protective arms around the little bay, and gorgeous flowering bushes and trees completed the heavenly appearance of the place. Unable to resist, Rachel took another wondering step out onto the beach. "I had no idea places like this really existed."

"Yeah, it's a beautiful place." Logan sounded thoughtful. "I come here when I need some quiet."

"You come here?" She tilted her head inquiringly. "Your friend Jake is pretty generous, huh?" As she spoke, she kicked off her shoes, wanting to feel the sand between her toes. Only when she turned back to him did she realize he'd fallen silent. She frowned. "You okay?"

"Yeah." He took her hand, a gallant smile on his face as he led her toward the waterline. "Yeah. I'm fine."

She shrugged and surrendered herself to the luxurious feel of silken sand and warm water, willing for once to give up the coarser subjects of abandonment and loss.

****

He had come so close to admitting to her what he'd done to get her alone with him, but if he did, everything he'd accomplished so far would be lost. Earlier, when he'd mentioned rescue, she hadn't looked hopeful, which meant she didn't want to leave because she no longer wanted to go back to the life she'd been living and the death she'd no doubt already planned. He could almost see her losing her steadfast guard against him. As if it were as simple as pulling off her shoes so she could feel the sand between her toes.

He took her to the cove first, showing her the little sea creatures that hid in the calm waters. The spiny sea urchins fascinated her so much she waded into the shallow water, squatting and peering at them curiously. He wished he'd thought to have his team plant snorkeling equipment in the cabin so he could take her out further and show her the angelfish and rainbow grouper that inhabited the coral reefs just off shore. By the time he brought her to the sandy beach where it was safe to swim, he'd lost himself in her innocent wonder of the world around her. And when they returned from a refreshing swim in the uplifting saltwater of the sea, she collapsed willingly next to him, disregarding the sand that clung to her hair, seeming intent on soaking up all the good the sun and sand and surf had to offer her.

He rolled over on his side, studying the relaxed way she lay, the way her mouth curved just slightly upward at the corners. A smile but as if she wasn't really thinking about it.

Her eyes were closed, her breath easy. She might have been asleep. He stroked a salty strand of hair back from her face, and her eyes fluttered open. "I like you like this."

"Like how?" She raised her eyebrows.

He searched for a word, finally landing on one that came closer than any other. "Free."

Her brow furrowed a little, but she didn't seem to want to reject the thought. "Free." She repeated it thoughtfully, then sat up, looking around her. Sand coated her perfect shoulder, dripped from her hair, made her look like some goddess who'd just emerged—fully formed but innocent—from the beach. "Maybe it's this place. I don't know if I've ever been free before. There's always somebody with some expectation of you. But not here. Here there's just the beach. And nobody expects anything out of you and you can just be." She smiled at him. "Maybe that's what makes it special. Is that why you came here?"

He hesitated, wondering how much he told her now would be a lie and how much that would damage her later on. Because she would know his lie eventually. She would have to be shown the trick because the woman he loved couldn't be a mark forever. But what she said was true, even for him. In this place he could be himself. In the jungle, there were no lies. "Yeah." His voice came out rough and he cleared his throat.

"After Nora...died. I came here a lot. Just to...clear it all away. This is where I fell in love with the islands, where I decided I never wanted to go back."

"And no regrets, right?" She sighed, wrapping her arms around her knees, gazing out at the hazy blue skyline. "God, it would be so wonderful. To find a place like this where I can just be, you know? No guilt, no past, no present even. Just me. Like I am right now." She laughed, turning her head toward him, her gaze encompassing him with its clarity. "Maybe here I could put the pieces back together. At least the ones I still want."

"How do you mean?"

"I mean I had everything. Other women envied me. I was on the top of every list, the first to be invited everywhere. Because of my husband, because of my status. And I lost it all." She shrugged, looking back at the horizon. "And right now I don't even care. I'm me right now and it's enough."

It was what he'd needed her to say all along, but he felt the tenuousness of it. Like a single strand of a spider web that when it broke would bring down the entire structure. If he pulled too hard, he'd bring down all the morning's gains.

Before he could decide how to proceed, she continued. "It sucks, you know? The way some women tear each other down. You've met my sister." She smiled a little as she placed her head on her knees, facing him so he could see her humorless smile. "We were so close as kids. But she always wanted what I had. My doll, my blouse. My husband." Her face hardened and he wanted to reach for her but held back, some instinct telling him not to touch her.

"It wasn't just her, though. It was all of them. The way they looked at me after—" She shot him a look that told him she wasn't quite ready to trust him yet. After a second, she continued. "And the gossip. Not that I minded them talking about me. That I could handle. It was the way they whispered when my back was turned, when they thought I couldn't hear. Up front they were all smiles and sympathy, but when I turned away, they whispered." She laughed, a harsh sound. "What would they think of me now, do you think? What would they whisper now?" Her face flushed and he knew she wasn't as shameless as she pretended.

How much of the past few months did she even remember? Between the alcohol and whatever grief haunted her, he wasn't sure there was much left except guilt. Impulsively, he reached for her hand. "We all do things after we've been hurt that we wouldn't normally do, you know."

She shook her head, a little smile on her lips. "That's just it. I don't think I ever knew who I really was...before. And now, well, who am I to say that was me or not? Maybe I'm the slut my sister thinks I am."

"I don't think she thinks you're a slut."

"And I don't care what she thinks I am." Her voice fell flat in the space between them. She squeezed his hand as if in apology and pulled away. "That's what I needed. To feel that I don't care. Even if I love her, even if she's all the family I have left, I don't care what she thinks. Here and now, I am. I could go swimming or run on the beach or just lay here with you all day burning in the tropical sun and I could honestly say I don't give a damn what she'd think of my decision. Or any of them, for that matter."

Her voice was rebellious, almost petulant, and he knew what she said wasn't true. She did care and what she really needed was to admit it. The pain would always be a factor as long as she held on to it. She had to let it all go and to do that she needed to forgive herself. And if she couldn't forgive those closest to her, how could she expect to forgive herself?

He sat up next to her, not touching her, wondering for the first time if what she needed was really within reach. He couldn't keep her here more than another day or two. Her sister would get suspicious if she couldn't get her on the phone. His friends were good, but he wasn't sure how long they could keep her at bay with half-truths and misdirection. If I have to tell her too soon, if I have to let her go back, it'll be for nothing. She'll hate me and she'll still hate herself and there'll be nothing I can do about it.

"Hey, why so serious?" She poked him, a playful smile on her lips. "We're here in paradise and nobody cares, right?"

He searched for a half-truth, something to cover up his real concern. Unable to respond in any other way, he leaned over and kissed her gently on the lips. "We're here, yes. And I like it here with you. But eventually someone will find us."

A shadow flitted across her face, as if a cloud had briefly covered the tropical sun. Then she shrugged. "Yeah, I guess. I mean, we can't be far from your island, right?"

"Not far at all. And they'll know we're missing by now."

"And you've got people who'll be looking for you."

"If only because it's easier than waiting seven years to declare me dead." He made his voice light. "Besides, you've got people who care about you, too. Your sister, for instance." He held up a hand when she opened her mouth to protest. "I know, I know. And I'm not saying I like her or that you should forgive her, but she did fly down the minute she knew you were here. She's not likely to give up on you now."

She closed her mouth with a snap and nodded, then she stood and pulled him to his feet. "All the more reason to enjoy paradise while we have it, then."

"What did you have in mind?" He quirked an eyebrow, doing his best not to put his arms around her.

She laughed. "How about another swim? Think you can catch me?"

The invitation was irresistible and he accepted it willingly, splashing after her through the clear water and wishing he could see through the path he'd chosen as easily as he could see through the water of the Caribbean.

****

By the time they returned to the cabin, Rachel was exhausted, her body literally tired of having fun. She leaned her head on Logan's arm. It felt good having a tall, strong man beside her to lean on. A clean good, though, unmarred by the sins of the past few weeks. Was it possible he was right? Could she heal? In that moment, she actually felt it might happen.

But he didn't know the whole story either. And what would change in the way he looked at her when he knew what she'd done?

She shook the thought off with a shudder and he glanced at her. "Are you all right?" He put his arm around her waist and she closed her eyes.

"Yeah. Yeah, I'm fine. Just...tired. I might lie down for a while if that's all right." She bit her lip.

"Sure. I've got a couple of steaks defrosting. If they're ready, I'll throw them on the grill in an hour or so, but you've got plenty of time. Go ahead and lie down."

She nodded and turned away, her heart sounding loud in her ears as she squeezed his hand and started for the bedroom. She closed the door and sat on the edge of the bed without removing her swimsuit and jeans. For several minutes she stared vacantly into the distance and then she gave up on holding back the tide of emotion and memory encroaching on her.

...the heavy traffic...the piercing sun...her head ached...she reached for the visor... She pulled away from the memory, but she could still feel the horror. That moment of terror would stay with her for the rest of her life, if only because of the shame she still felt at her own weakness. *Dear God, no wonder Kevin couldn't look at me.* Self-loathing choked her until she forced herself to take a breath, to suck it in past the anguish. *If I'd only been in control. If I'd just kept my cool...*

But I wasn't in control. I lost my baby because I wasn't in control. She put a hand on her now flat stomach. Dear God, was it possible she'd ever carried a baby there for seven months? Almost long enough. But so far away from the final goal it didn't even matter. Close only counts in horseshoes and hand grenades.

The days after the accident had been horrible. Everyone knew. Her baby was dead and it was all her own fault. The platitudes and offered solace tore holes in her soul and left her bleeding in places that couldn't be mended. And Kevin, the one person she'd thought she could count on for anything, wasn't there for her. Because he blamed her, too.

Anger and pain and the terrible guilt bore down on her again and she curled up on the bed in a fetal position and let the darkness take her.

****

Logan stole into the bedroom half an hour later to cover her with a light blanket. He paused when he noticed the tear tracks on her cheeks. He wanted to brush those tears away, but he knew he needed to get to the dock, to reassure Tony or Andre. Whoever was waiting there for him. He needed to beg them to buy him more time, even one more day. One more day to work whatever magic the island was willing to lend him.

He noticed the wind had risen a little as he approached the dock. Two figures waited there, hair streaming, clothes pressed against their bodies as if by a large hand. He expected

Tony. His friend was worried about the whole experiment and what the consequences might be. The slight female figure next to Tony confused him at first, but as he neared the dock, he quickened his step, a grin widening on his lips. "Sabrina! I didn't know you were coming down." He swept the little woman into a hug and she laughed.

"You didn't think I was going to miss the greatest magic trick in any of our careers, did you? Seriously, Logan, I can't believe you pulled it off." As he set her down, she craned her neck to look up at him. "God, you're so freaking tall."

"No taller than last time." He smiled down at her. Sabrina, at four foot eleven inches and about a hundred pounds, was one of the biggest personalities he'd ever known. Nothing about her was small in spite of her diminutive form. A special effects engineer—perhaps the special effects engineer as far as magic went—for many Hollywood movies, this was not the first magic trick she'd advised him on.

"And that's been far too long," she replied tartly. "There are movies just waiting for your touch, Logan. When are you coming back? Is this the beginning of it?"

Coming back. God no. To the life he'd led with Nora? The dreams he'd promised her? "No."

His voice must have come out more harshly than he'd intended because she recoiled and he groaned inwardly. "No. I mean—I'm retired, Sabrina. Really. Maybe Andre could—" He glanced at Tony, who shrugged.

"I'm more concerned with you ending up in jail and taking me and Andre with you." Tony glanced at Sabrina. "Not to mention you and your crew. If no one else has noticed, I have. We're all accessories to a crime here."

"She won't press charges." Logan shoved his hands into his pockets and turned to Tony. "Look. I'm sorry I dragged you guys into this. If you need to leave, I understand. I've got the satellite phone and can call for a helicopter at any time. You can walk away clean. But I'm making progress with her. It's working. This place. I swear to you, it will help her. I just need more time."

Tony looked reluctant, but he finally nodded. "How much?"

"A day. Maybe two."

His friend looked at his feet. "There's a storm on the way." He said it with the tone of a man pulling the last shell out of his arsenal.

The rise in the wind made more sense. Logan peered at the sky but it seemed clear. "How bad?"

"It's not supposed to be bad, but you know how that is around here, Logan, especially on these smaller islands. According to reports, it'll be here tomorrow evening, and it'll have straight-line winds up to 30 miles per hour. But that could mean it'll arrive at noon with 65 mile per hour winds. You just can't be certain. And it's her life as well as yours you have to take into account."

Logan nodded, thinking. "I understand your concern, but the cabin's withstood hurricanes. We're off the beach and protected by the jungle from the worst of it. Those trees have stood for centuries. Anything less than a hurricane isn't going to convince me to leave. Not when I'm this close." He glanced at Sabrina again. "So, what do you think? You able to orchestrate our 'rescue' day after tomorrow?"

"It'll cost you, but I know you're good for it." She grinned. "And for the record, I mean, I don't know this chick, but if you're willing to move heaven and earth for her like this…well, she's one lucky woman."

Did her voice actually sound wistful? He'd known Sabrina for years, worked with her, knew her ambitions and that she was the youngest of four and the only girl, that she liked her coffee strong and sweet and that she'd never had time for relationships. How much had the last few years changed her, though?

Before he could react, she'd moved on, turning to indicate a small box on the bench. "Brought you some goodies."

She flashed him a smile and a wink. "In case the island and your charm aren't enough."

"Yeah, thanks." He struggled to regain his bearings and helped her into the boat. The water that had been so calm on the other side of the island was getting choppy. When he turned back to Tony, he caught his friend's worried look and nodded. "I get it, okay? I'll keep an eye on the weather. And I have the satellite phone if things get too bad."

Tony nodded, a look of relief plain on his face. "Okay. Deal. And I'm going to use my discretion, too. Just remember, if you let it go too long, we won't be able to get to you until after it's over. And then there may not be time to stage any dramatic rescues. The real one might be all we've got."

Chapter 9

Logan returned to the cottage before dark, secreting the little box of supplies Sabrina had given him under the kitchen sink. He stood to find Rachel in the bedroom door, yawning, her eyes still closed. He stepped away from the sink. "Hey. Feel better?"

She dropped her arms to her sides, her expression unreadable. "Not sure I'd go that far. Were you outside? I thought I heard the door close."

"Just checking the weather. Looks like a storm coming." He narrowed his eyes, studying her. Something was different and he suspected it had to do with the tears he'd seen earlier. Deciding not to push, he added as he turned casually, "Won't be here before tomorrow, I don't think."

She nodded. "Good." Her gaze wandered, her expression vacant. "I don't want a storm now."

He didn't like the look on her face and he stepped forward. "I've been thinking...maybe you should learn tai chi."

Her eyes turned back to him, dark in the evening light. "Why would I do that?"

"It's a great way to....pass the time." He didn't want to say "release tension" because it seemed to hit too close to a mark he'd tried to avoid. "I'm not an instructor, but I could teach you a few basic moves. We could do it together in the morning."

"Are you worried I'm going to get bored?" Her lips twisted with humor, which was not what he was going for, but much better than vacancy. She raised her eyebrows. "Let's see, plane crash, jungle hike, excellent dinner last night, first taste of Scotch, swimming in a private lagoon today... Nope. Haven't been bored yet."

"You haven't had a chance yet." He moved behind her and placed his hands on her hips, feeling her tense. "Relax. I'm not going to hurt you."

"I never thought you would." Her voice sounded like taut guitar strings.

"Good." He left his hands on her hips and moved close enough so his lips were almost against her right ear. "Push your hips forward a little and bend your legs. Feels kind of like you're getting ready to sit down. Not squatting, just a subtle bend in your posture."

"This might go better if I'd had a shower and changed my clothes since our swim." Her voice sounded a little breathless and he smiled. Her response reassured him she wasn't retreating into depression. He led her through a couple of introductory moves, moving in concert with her, concentrating as hard as he could on the peaceful sensation of the exercise, willing it to pass from his body to hers.

She adapted to the gentle motion of the tai chi easily, as he'd known she would. Within minutes, they were moving together, several inches separating them, but somehow bound together in a rhythm he'd felt flowing through him earlier as he stood on the edge of the jungle. As they paused at the end of the last movement, he felt the skin of his palm tingle with longing to broach the space and touch her. He stepped back. "Great. That'll get you started. Now all you have to do is get up early enough tomorrow to practice with me."

She glanced over her shoulder, expression eager for praise. "How'd I do?"

He pretended to consider. "It'll get easier."

"What?" She blinked, startled.

"The moves. The more you do them, the easier they get." He kept a straight face.

"You didn't like the way I did them?"

He snorted. "You're not going to master tai chi in one day, sweetheart. Doesn't matter how devoted to the art you are."

"Maybe I'm not looking to master tai chi." She crossed her arms over her chest petulantly.

"I don't know of many things you can master in one day."

Her stance changed as if he'd issued a challenge. She grinned. "No matter how devoted to the art you are?" She looped her arms around his neck and pulled him in for a kiss.

Caught off guard—again—by her innate sensuality, he'd already responded, pulling her firmly against him, enjoying the taste and feel of her, his heart still synchronized to hers from the tai chi. But the niggling voice in his head wouldn't stop whispering that she wasn't healed...no way had one day of relaxation set her on the right path. She was using him the same way she had used the college kid and who knew how many others...to fill a void left by some as yet unexplained sorrow. His lips still locked with hers, he summoned all his strength, captured her hands and pulled them down to his heart, holding them tightly even as he took advantage of the small space he'd created between them and stepped away, shaking his head. "Sorry. I can't."

"Why the ever living hell not?" Her frustration was evident. She yanked away. "I'm obviously willing." She stepped forward and slid her hands under his t-shirt, palms flat against his skin. "God, Logan. I want you. I don't know how much plainer I can be. And you keep kissing and teasing and never following through…" She shook her head. "Jeez."

He closed his eyes, aware of how very much he really wanted to follow through with her, but he couldn't risk damaging her that way. She was so used to men either betraying her or taking advantage of her, she couldn't comprehend that he could want her and still hold back. "I do want you." When she rolled her eyes, he took her hands, reluctantly removing them from his body. "The timing needs to be right, though. I truly do want to make love to you, but this— this just isn't it."

"Because of my 'self-destructive path'?" She grinned humorlessly at him.

"No. Because I'm responsible for you being here." He spoke without thinking, still a little off balance. At her quizzical look, he groaned. "I mean that it was my responsibility to get you to Cancun safely and I failed. I screwed up."

"It was a mechanical problem. That's not your fault." She shrugged. "So we might as well make the most of our time—"

"No. I'm sorry." He squeezed her hands and turned away, releasing her and going into the kitchen to take the steaks he'd put in to marinade out of the fridge.

When he turned back, she stood with her arms crossed over her chest. He raised his eyebrows, better able to continued his manufactured lie now he was several feet away from her. "It can't be helped, Rachel. And as much as I'd like to believe for certain it's not my fault, there's always pilot error to take into account. And if it is my fault you're here, taking advantage of you—just isn't right."

She considered his words for a moment, then groaned, looking at the ceiling. "You had to put me on a deserted island with a sexy, honorable man?" She glanced back at him, a little smile on her lips. "Fine, but as soon as we're off this island—"

"I won't be responsible for what happens then." He grinned, hoping this meant she had accepted his excuse.

"Good. I'm going to take a shower. And if you change your mind and want to join me…" Her wicked smile seemed to indicate she hadn't given up.

He sank onto the couch, exhausted from fighting his own instincts and desires. He had a feeling it was a battle he would soon lose. He considered the box under the sink, but rejected it. It didn't feel right. Like cheating. Turning resolutely to the plate glass window, he considered the jungle and a peaceful feeling came over him. He didn't need magic tricks and special effects. Not here. Because this was where magic lived. And that was the only kind of magic that could ever heal Rachel.

****

After dinner, they sat on the patio, feet propped on the edge of the hot tub while they reclined in the soft chairs. The insects and small animals rattled and clicked and chirped in a cacophony of background noise that Rachel tried mentally to decipher, as impossible a task as unwinding one instrument in a symphony from another. The wind had risen, but so far it amounted to just enough breeze to keep the heat of the night and the bugs at bay. The dishes from another excellent meal still sat on the table behind them. She sipped her wine. "I keep forgetting I'm stuck here."

He didn't answer at first, and she wondered if he'd heard her, but then he stood and walked over to the edge of the patio. "I used to wish I could get stuck here. I've always loved this place. It's where I first started to heal after…"

"Nora." She nodded. "Did you come here to stay with Jake?"

"Jake." He glanced over his shoulder, and his expression made her wonder if there was bad blood between him and his friend. Surely nothing else could account for the odd mix of emotions that passed over his face. "Yeah, he didn't own the place then. I guess you could say I'm kind of responsible for him owning it now. I came here wanting to bury myself. I didn't think I could ever get over the guilt. I wanted to be completely alone, isolated, because I didn't think I belonged with humans anymore." His gaze wandered back out toward the jungle. "But then something funny happened. I felt something out here. Something sort of healing and soothing and wild all at the same time. I still think it's magic. Real magic, not the kind I did on the stage."

"Real magic?" Her incredulity was instant, but faded when he turned to face her. "Really?"

He shrugged. "I'm sure it's different things to different people, but I'm also certain I'm not the only one who has felt it. The Mayans built their temples in the middle of the jungle. Even now, there are spas and new age healing centers springing up in rainforests everywhere." His lip curled a little with distaste, and she wondered why. Wasn't that pretty much what he'd done with his resort on a Caribbean island? Even though she knew the resort emphasized recycling and conservation, such a large place must leave a pretty big footprint on the ecosystem. But then she looked around her at the largely unspoiled smaller island and understood.

"This is what you wanted, wasn't it? This little island? But why not buy it? Why build the resort on the big island instead?"

"Because I had a dream, I guess. I wanted to share it, help other people." He laughed. "Don't get me wrong. My resort is wonderful. I feel I share some of the magic I found here, and that's important to me. Magic always has been something I like to share, and it's possible there. But here, it's like it's...more immediate. Like I can really feel what the magic is in its natural form. And I don't think you're going to find that in a spa or a resort."

She nodded, thinking about the sounds of the jungle again. She'd barely noticed them at the resort, but they were so close here. One birdsong twining into another, insects and small animals chirping and the whole air swelling with life. No, this magic couldn't be appreciated from a resort setting, but here at this little cottage, it was inescapable. She had a haunting feeling that Logan, in this state of mind at least, was a part of it, and that it could overcome her, too, if she let it.

A howler monkey scream split the air and she jerked upright. "I think I'm going to go to bed." He nodded, his eyes still very far away, and she put her hand on his shoulder, at least partly to reassure herself he was really still there. He turned his head and kissed her wrist lightly, sending a shiver down her spine, and she reclaimed her hand and hurried inside.

****

Logan stayed outside for several minutes after she went to bed, his feet propped on the hot tub, feeling more stuck in one place than he had for a while. His brain wouldn't stop thinking about Nora and what he might have done to keep her happy and alive. He'd failed Nora and Jasmine, and he feared he would fail Rachel, too.

Another howler monkey scream cut through the rising wind, seemingly right beside the house although he knew it was probably miles away. Startled in spite of himself, he jerked out of his trance. His fears wouldn't do anyone any good. The jungle was trying to tell him something. He straightened, listening, then stood to gather the plates from dinner to carry into the kitchen before turning in.

The scream that pierced the air wasn't a monkey this time. He recognized Rachel's voice, and he dropped the plates, hearing them smash on the tile behind him, but he was already inside, yanking the bedroom door open, and she spilled into his arms, clad only in a t-shirt, her body shaking, her face white.

"Rachel!" Half angry, half frightened, he shook her a little. "God, what happened?"

"In the...in the bathroom." She gasped the words, obviously in a state of shock.

Wondering if a snake had gotten into the cottage— which did sometimes happen although he'd had it built as airtight as possible—he deposited her on the couch and crept into the bathroom. The light was on and he spotted the culprit almost immediately. A large, colorful spider, almost as big as his palm, had invaded and made itself at home on the mirror. He recognized it as a harmless garden spider and carefully swiped it into a cup to transport outside.

He came back, displaying the empty cup with a flourish. "There you are, madam. One spider eliminated and no harm done. He'll be happier in the jungle anyway." He paused, concern overcoming his attempt at lightheartedness. "It was completely harmless, I promise. Are you all right?"

Stupid question. She sat on the sofa, hugging her knees to her chest, tears on her cheeks and her eyes downcast. She turned her haunted gaze to him. "That's what they told me."

"Who told you?"

"Them. Kevin. Angel. About the wolf spider." Her voice assumed a different cadence as if she were mimicking someone. "They're harmless, Rach. It wouldn't have hurt you, but you had to go and freak out because a spider fell on you and now…" Her voice broke. "It was all my fault. They were right. I did it. I reached for my sunglasses while I was driving, and the spider fell out on me. That's how the accident happened. That's how I lost my baby."

So that's what she lost. Comprehension dawned on him and he sat on the couch next to her. "Oh my God. Oh, sweetheart." And her husband and sister had blamed her. Rage filled him but he suppressed it, gathering her into his arms. "And you feel responsible."

"Of course I do." Her body felt rigid, refusing the comfort he offered, and he backed off. She glared at him. "I am responsible. I panicked, my muscles seized up, I practically forgot I was driving and I ran into a telephone pole. The doctors told me I had a 'cardiac incident', probably partly due to the pregnancy, because my blood pressure had been high enough to be watched. Not high enough to put me on bed rest, but they were monitoring it." She looked at her hands, still clasped over her knees, and her savage voice calmed in an ominous way. "The doctor said it was a combination of things, really, that killed my baby. The cardiac incident, blunt trauma from the accident, and who knows what all else. But I know it was really me." Something behind her face broke, giving him a glimpse behind her guard. Her hands opened and closed in a convulsive, grasping motion. "My baby...I killed him."

"No." He thought about how such a simple thing had turned her life into a tragedy. Just a harmless spider. Probably another ten minutes and she would have been safe at home, her baby still growing inside her. And now she'd be a happy mother with an adoring husband instead of heartbroken, alone and trying to ruin what was left of her life.

It's the same for me, really. If I'd been there more often, maybe I would've known how much Nora needed me. And we'd be a happy family with Jasmine right now. The difference, he knew, was that although he still felt responsible for his wife's death, he'd accepted the fact that though he probably would feel regret for the rest of his life, he could continue to live. How could he help Rachel do the same?

He took her hands, giving them a little tug, and this time she didn't resist; she unfolded like a blanket and came to rest against him. He stroked her dark hair, remembering her as she'd been before Nora's death, how Nora had always said Rachel was the only one who could cheer her up. He wished he'd known her better then, but he might not be holding her now if he had.

How could her sister and husband betray her? How could they not be there for her when she needed them most? If his own friends had deserted him after Nora's death, he wasn't sure he would have fared as well. In fact, however, Tammy had staunchly defended him, Tony and Andre had been true, even Nora's family, although they'd never totally forgiven him for not being there, didn't blame him any more than they blamed themselves.

"Sweetheart, you have to let it go. It's eating you up from the inside out, and I can't stand to see it happen. You have so much to offer the world still, and you have to find a way to move on."

"Eating me up?" Her voice choked on itself and her entire body shuddered. "God, it's like that. It's like a black hole in me. Like it's eating everything that once made me what I am supposed to be. I can't even…I can't even feel sorry for the things I've done. I know it's been wrong, using people the way I do. I know it but nothing seems to matter when I think that I'll never be able to hold my son, never talk to him, never—" She broke off, swallowing her own voice with a gulp, her body still shaking.

He tightened his arm around her shoulders, looking for some comfort to offer her. He finally found it in the words his own mother had said after Nora's death. He didn't often think of her in connection with Nora because she'd held her distance. He knew she resented the way he felt about his part in Nora's death. She didn't think he was responsible for Nora's actions and she'd been rather outspoken about it.

"Son, you can't do this to yourself. She made a decision. Yes, she was sick and the Lord will take that into account, but her actions are not yours. And in the end, who's to say it wasn't what was meant to be?"

Meant to be. God, he'd hated his mother for a second after she'd said that. How could such a thing be meant to be? He'd forbidden her coming to the funeral, had given Jasmine to Nora's mother, had banished himself. He still only spoke to his mother on a monthly basis. But when he stopped to think about it, maybe she was right. Maybe it had been God's plan for him to lose Nora and be here to help Rachel.

But how to say such a thing to her? It was absurd to a lonely, heartbroken woman. He took a deep breath and tilted her chin up so he could see her face. Her gaze met his and he knew he had to try to find a way.

He took a deep breath, let it out and let his own faith guide his words. "You know that thing people say after a tragedy happens? The one you hate? That maybe it was meant to be?"

She flinched. He nodded. "Yeah. I always felt like that too. I hated the people who would say that to me. I hated the idea that God could have such a horrible plan." He stroked her hair back from her face. "I never believed it, either. Not until right now."

"No." She shook her head and pulled away, but she didn't leave him. Though she was rejecting his words, she wasn't pushing away from him. "Don't say God had to take Nora away because I would need you."

He shook his head. "No. That's not what I mean. I loved Nora. And I don't blame God or you. And I'll never, ever not feel responsible for failing her. But..." He hesitated, then shrugged. "I'm not in charge, you know? I made bad decisions. I carry my guilt. But until this moment, I never wanted to think that my guilt and my bad decisions and my grief were just a part of the bigger picture. It's a really big picture, you know. Bigger than you, me, Nora, Jasmine..." He put his hands on either side of her face, framing it. "And your baby. And even your sister and— God help him   your husband. When you think of all the pain and suffering and beauty and happiness and horror and everything else that happens in the world every second, it makes you feel kind of small, doesn't it? Somewhere a baby is being born, somewhere someone is dying, somewhere someone is falling in love and someone else is saying good-bye." He shook his head. "It's too big and too complex for us to figure out how our little pieces fit into it. All we have is just you and me and, if we can find it, a little faith that whatever happens, if we're trying to do right, it'll be enough."

She was silent for several seconds. Again, she pulled away, but she stayed on the couch, facing away from him, toward the room. Outside he could hear the wind howling in the jungle. When did that happen? The storm must be getting here sooner than Tony had anticipated. But he couldn't worry about that now. All he could do was wait.

****

Rachel didn't want to think Logan's words were right. She didn't want to believe in her own redemption. She'd spent so much time condemning herself for her baby's death, echoing what she heard from Kevin and Angel, she couldn't believe there might be a way out for her.

"I don't..." She put her hand on her belly, feeling the emptiness there. She lifted her eyes to Logan. "Logan, I can't believe that."

"You mean you can't let yourself believe it." He nodded. "I understand, but you can. Just let go, baby. Let it go and let yourself be free of the pain. If you were wrong, believe that you've been forgiven and it'll be easier to forgive yourself."

"It feels like cheating." She whispered the words, almost ashamed she was even thinking of it.

"But it's not." He smiled, and she recognized a peace in his expression that she'd never seen there before. "It's acceptance. I don't think I ever realized what that meant. The final stage of grief, right? Accept the loss, I always thought. But that's not it. It's accepting your role in life. Accepting that some higher power—God, I guess—has a reason for taking something away and leaving you here. And as much as you'd like to take the weight of the world on your own shoulders, it's not your job to do that."

In spite of herself, she felt something, an emotion she hadn't allowed in her heart for so long it took her a moment to comprehend what it was. Hope.

Like a pinprick of light, a tiny flame a long way away...a star in the palm of her hand. Hope.

If she could let go of the guilt, would living still be possible for her? Yes, her body was empty now, but her heart still might have the capacity to be filled with love. If she let the light of hope take over the darkness in her soul—if she sought and received forgiveness and accepted that there was still a place for her in the patchwork quilt of God's plan—what might be possible for her?

"Logan—" She whispered his name through trembling lips, but he stopped her.

"Say my name." His expression was filled with both tense anticipation and dread. "Call me by my first name."

She sucked in a startled breath. No one had dared call him Ian since Nora died. In the first few months after Nora's death, his given name had been met with a cold glare and "Call me Logan." He'd given up his name, part of his penance for being someone she couldn't count on in the end. The honor of being the one he asked to end that punishment made her hesitate.

"Please." He took her hands. "I haven't wanted to hear it until now. But I want you to say it. Call me by my name and help me start over, Rachel."

The world had frozen around them. Waiting, perhaps to change direction. For both of them. She'd never been more conscious of a word in her life. It rose in her throat and hovered there for a moment until she released it, a shining beacon for both of them. "Ian." The name tasted sweet on her tongue, easier to utter than she'd anticipated. She smiled a little in relief and lifted a hand to touch his face. "Ian."

His smile answered hers, and then he leaned forward, kissing her, at first very gently, but then he pulled her into his arms and lap and she gave herself up to him as he explored her mouth with his tongue. Her breath hitched in her chest, but more important was the sudden ferocious need to be as close to him as possible, as if that alone could convince her what he said about a new beginning was true.

After what might have been several minutes, an hour or just a few seconds, she felt him stand, still holding her. She looped her arms around his neck, lips grazing his jaw. A sound from outside made her stiffen a little. "What was that?"

She felt the bed beneath her and his body warm on top of her. "Just the wind." He kissed her again, his hands beneath the t-shirt on her sides, caressing. She arched up against him and he laughed.

"Is it storming?" She gasped the words, reaching for his shirt, not really caring about the weather outside when what was happening in her own heart was so much more important.

He drew away, kissing the end of her nose, his hands cupping her breasts as he tilted his head as if listening. He smiled down at her. "Not anymore."

The wind howled again, and a branch smacked against the window, contradicting his words, but she didn't even flinch. Instead, she reached up for another kiss, lips eager for his, but found herself hesitating at the last minute.

He seemed to sense her withdrawal and paused. "What's wrong?"

"I just—" She stumbled and blushed a little. "I don't know how to...how to do this anymore. Not this way."

"Is it going too fast?" He brushed her hair out of her face. "It's okay. I'll stop."

"No." She caught him before he could roll off her, winding her legs through his. "God no. Don't leave. It's just that I've...had sex with a lot of guys—"

He raised his eyebrows. "I am not certain this is helping the mood."

"—but it's been a long time since it's mattered. I want it to be different but I'm not sure how to do that anymore."

Comprehension softened his expression. "How about I show you?"

"Can you?" Her breath came faster at the thought.

He answered by sitting up, somehow pulling her t-shirt from her body with a deft twist of his hand. She would have sat up too, but he shook his head, pushing her back onto the blankets. "Just lie there. I want to look at you."

She closed her eyes, self-conscious beneath his gaze. He laughed. "Feeling shy?" Clothing rustled and she felt his lips on her neck, his bare chest against hers. She trembled and he moved his lips to her ear. "It's okay to want me, baby."

"I don't know if it is." She swallowed hard. "I haven't...haven't wanted anything this much since..." Had she ever wanted anyone this much? Even in the early days of her relationship with Kevin, had it been like this?

"Shh." He lay next to her, turning her on her side to face him. "Open your eyes." When she did, he pulled her closer and she realized he'd discarded more than his shirt. Her gaze fluttered down, a wanton desire to see him allowing her to admire his lean hips and long legs. God, he was tan all over. Did he have a tanning bed or did he run naked on the beach when he wanted?

The idea made her smile and when she looked back at him she found him watching her, his expression a mixture of amusement and arousal, but the amusement faded into tenderness when their eyes met. He caressed a tendril of hair, pushing it back over her ear and sliding his hand back to the nape of her neck. His eyes on hers, he spoke in a soft voice. "Are you certain?"

She felt as if her heart was in her mouth, preventing speech. The time for words was past anyway. Their bodies pressed together as if of their own accord, she wrapped one leg around his hips and pulled him even closer, feeling his erection pressing against her. A slight movement by either of them and he'd be inside her. She held her breath and nodded. She expected him to enter her then, but he didn't. Instead, he continued kissing her, very gently, moving a little away to work his hands between them, caressing her breasts, moving lower over her belly to the soaking spot between her legs, fingers sliding into her effortlessly.

She arched her back, surprised by the onslaught in spite of herself. His low laughter rumbled in her ear. Was he laughing at her? She thought of all the magic she'd already seen him accomplish with those fingers—catching the star, producing a rose. Was it any wonder he found all her secrets so quickly, massaged and teased and stroked until she cried out with an animalistic passion she'd all but forgotten she was capable of and she clung to him as her orgasm swept through her, emptying her, leaving her clean and drifting on a wave of remembered pleasure.

She barely noticed he'd rolled them over, covering her body with his. Her heart rate sped up and she felt her attention refocus. Broad shoulders, well-defined chest tapering to a flat stomach… Dear God, he was magnificent. And she did want him. When he slid his knee between her legs and she let them part for him, she realized it went beyond that, though.

She needed him, and when her eyes met his, she knew he knew she needed him, beyond want or desire or even reason.

He bent his head, kissing her deeply, and she wound her arms around his neck, kissing him back with total abandon. He was right. In spite of all she'd lost and all she'd done, she could be whole again in his arms.

He pulled away for a moment, searching for something. He didn't have to go far to find it, and she heard the soft crinkle of the condom wrapper with a smile. Either he knew his friend Jake better than he'd said, or she was not the first woman he'd seduced here. Not that it mattered. The only thing that mattered was what was between the two of them now. So much more than sex or seduction.

He needs me too. Her heartbeat quickened and she reached for the condom wrapper. He held it out of her reach for a moment, and she was temporarily distracted by the perfection of his arm. Smooth, sun-bronzed skin over well-defined muscles. She let her reaching hand trail along the biceps and pectorals she'd been admiring and he laughed, seizing her around the waist and flipping her over so she straddled him. Then, kissing her, he gave her the condom. "Put it on me."

The four words were both invitation and order, and she had no intention of refusing either. She tore the wrapper with her teeth, but, her heart beating in her throat, she caressed his erection with her free hand, holding the condom in the other. He moaned, arching his back and moving against her stroking hand, giving her a sense of utter power until he opened his eyes and fixed her with a stern glare. "If you don't put that damn thing on me right now, I'm going to take you without it."

The thought of making love to him without barriers made her heart stop, but after the promiscuous lifestyle she'd led the past few weeks, she couldn't swear she was safe. She'd hardly worried about safe sex on the course of her self-destruction, though some of her partners had taken the initiative. For the first time, she wished she'd taken more care.

His hands moved to her waist, and he half lifted her, positioning himself beneath her. "Now, baby." His voice urged her to action. "Do it now."

Obediently, she rolled the condom over him and almost as soon as she'd done it, he released her and thrust upward at the same moment. The sensation of fullness made her gasp and bend over, her long hair falling in a veil over them. She shook it off, impatient, wanting to see his face, to know it meant as much to him as it did to her.

"God, you feel so good." He half-whispered the words, holding her hips firmly with both hands again, grinding against her as if to bury himself further into her. He held her there for a moment, then let her go, watching as she raised her hips, then catching her and pulling her back, meeting her halfway with his thrust and holding her again before releasing her to repeat the movement.

He continued the sweet torture, and each thrust built the fire inside her, until all she wanted was to ride him until she could explode and ease the excruciating pressure of pleasure. "Please." She felt the sweat of restraint break out over her skin. "God, please, Logan...Ian."

"Not yet." He was sweating, too, and he half sat up, curving one arm around her back, restraining her from the wild, breathless, galloping orgasm she longed for. "Not yet." He ground his hips against her again, and this time he groaned and held her still for a moment, then, just as she was certain she would truly spontaneously combust, right there in his arms, he released her and met each of her downward thrusts with an upward one, and it was all she needed to explode inside and come floating down in the embers into his arms as he called out her name like a prayer in the dark and came at last.

Chapter 10

Logan felt lighter than he had in a long while. As if he'd finally let some heavy load slide away. He wondered how he'd gotten through the days and weeks and years since Nora's death without this feeling in his life. Maybe he could have had it if he'd kept Jasmine. Maybe with his daughter in his life he could have let go of the guilt and anguish sooner.

Rachel lay silent in the crook of his arm, one hand on his chest. He wondered what she felt right then. Was it as much of a new start for her as it had been for him? Or did she regret letting him past her guard and into her heart? He covered the hand on his chest and when she looked up at him, he asked, "Are you all right?"

Her lazy smile of contentment reassured him. "I'm so much better than all right. I haven't felt like this...ever, I don't think." Her smile faded a little. "It was never like this with Kevin. We made love, we made plans, we started a life together, but it was never like we really belonged together. But...if it weren't for the accident, we'd still be together." Her voice faded.

"What happened, after the accident?" When she shot him a sharper look, he nodded. "I know your husband and your sister—but how?" How could he do that to you? How could he betray you?

She was silent for several seconds, then took a deep breath. "I know what you're thinking. That he was to blame. And yes, he was, for a lot of it. But I guess I'm starting to see how it happened."

"Tell me." He tightened his grip on her hand and she smiled, kissing him lightly before she continued.

"I shut him out. I didn't mean to, but I didn't deal with it the same way he did. The way everyone did. When they told me about my baby, I cried. All night. I thought it would rip me in half. And then in the morning, I—just couldn't anymore. I tried. God, I wanted to. But I couldn't. Everyone around me was crying and it was like this little black knot in my chest. I couldn't seem to let go of it. And the longer it stayed there, the bigger it got. Like the tears I couldn't cry were kind of feeding it." She sat very still, breathing hard. "And then Angel and Kevin—" she shot him a look that told him how much was still unresolved between the sisters.

"They had an affair." He nodded, wishing he dared touch her.

"I thought that's what it was when I caught them." She lowered her head again, her shoulders tense. "But it was more than that. They fell in love. They grieved for the baby together because I couldn't."

The wind rose outside and rain lashed the windows. She started a little. "How long has it been storming?"

"It's nothing to worry about." He remembered the smashed dinner plates and glasses on the patio. Oh well, the wind and rain would most likely take care of the mess now. He wondered how fast the wind gusts were. He'd guess at least forty miles an hour. But straight line winds were nothing much to worry about in a sturdy little cabin in a clearing. He kissed the top of her head, feeling drowsy now. "Try to sleep."

"Hmm." She snuggled closer, her naked body warm against his, accidentally making it more difficult for him to get comfortable. However, as she relaxed and her breathing deepened, he slipped into sleep too.

****

A crash outside woke Rachel with a start and she flung the covers back, leaping from the bed. Momentarily uncertain of her surroundings and caught by surprise by her own nakedness, she reached for a blanket to cover herself with but stopped when she caught sight of Logan by the window. He was naked, too, bringing back memories of making love to him. She relaxed. This was safe. Here, with him, she could rest.

"Logan? What's wrong? Is the storm worse?"

He came to her, putting his arms around her. "It's all right. Everything's fine."

She felt him harden against her and couldn't help a little giggle. "I'll say." She moved closer, sliding her hands between them to caress him. "What have you conjured up for me, magic man?"

He laughed hoarsely and spun her around onto the bed. Off balance, they fell onto it together, and he kissed her passionately and thoroughly before drawing away enough to whisper, just audible above the storm, "I think you're the magic one this time."

They made love again with the lightning, thunder and wind howling outside. But Rachel felt as if she'd never been more at peace than she was in his arms.

****

The sound of the jungle outside woke him. He lay listening for a few moments, thankful the storm had left the cabin untouched and hoping the jungle hadn't suffered too badly. He'd have to call Tony sooner rather than later, but he dreaded it. He wasn't even sure why until Rachel moved beside him and he knew. He'd have to call Tony to arrange for their "rescue". The ruse couldn't be kept up much longer, and there was no need for it, anyway. He wasn't the only one who had hit a reset button last night. Rachel was ready to face the rest of her life. But that meant it was time to tell her the truth, too.

But not yet. She slept so peacefully next to him he couldn't fathom how to tell her he'd deceived her. He couldn't even honestly be certain what her reaction would be. How could he have known about this woman's existence for nearly a decade—and now know her as intimately as it was possible to know her—but have no idea what her next action would be?

God, she was beautiful, though. Perfect, peaceful, a tendril of her dark hair curling over her flushed cheek. She smiled a little in her sleep and he thought about kissing her into wakefulness, caressing her into arousal and enjoying everything that followed—

"Are you going to kiss me or not?"

Startled, he jerked himself out of his reverie to find her looking at him, wide-eyed and awake. He snorted and poked her. "You were supposed to be asleep."

"I was waiting for you to wake me up. Properly." She gave him a demure smile.

He laughed out loud. "Properly? Really? Let's see if I can't just do that." He dove under the covers, catching her in the ticklish spots underneath her armpits that he'd discovered last night.

She jerked and squirmed. "No fair! Tickling isn't fair!"

"All's fair in love and war, sweetheart." He moved to cover her squirming body, letting her feel his arousal.

She froze beneath him. "Love and war?"

He didn't hesitate, brushing her hair from her face and kissing her gently. "Yeah. I wasn't always sure which one this thing between us was, but last night love won the battle, I think. I love you, Rachel."

She sucked in her breath. "I...love you, too, Ian."

He grinned. "I like the way you say my name."

"Do you?" She kissed his chin, then his cheek. "Ian."

"Logan!" The shout from the living room made him start and turn his head just as the door opened and Tony appeared, his face anxious.

Logan groaned and moved aside, felt Rachel sit up partway, remember her nudity and retreat beneath the blankets. "Tony? What the hell, man?" Confusion at his friend's appearance gave way to irritation. What was Tony doing here now? Hadn't they settled on one more day?

Tony's gaze took in the scene he'd walked in on and he stumbled a half step backward, looking a little embarrassed. "The storm...I was..."

Logan glanced over his shoulder. Rachel peeked out of the blankets, her expression still amused. She obviously just thought their rescue had come at an inopportune time. Logan wanted to kiss her one more time. God alone only knew if she'd let him in a few minutes.

"I'll, um, wait...out here."

The door closed behind Tony and Rachel emerged. She rolled her eyes. "Good timing, huh?"

"The best. He's not in the magic business for nothing." Logan chose his next words carefully. "We need to talk."

"About?" She sat up, brushing her hair back off her shoulders. "You think I have time to take a shower? I'd hate to hold up the rescue, but if there's going to be anyone taking pictures, I'd rather not look like I just tumbled out of bed..." She trailed off and gave him a sly grin. When he didn't answer it, her expression changed to one of concern. "Logan, it's okay. I know, I hate for this to end, too, but this—between us—it doesn't have to end. It'll take some doing, but we can be together, see if it works—" She broke off when he took her hands. "What? You're scaring me."

"We were never in a plane wreck."

"I know. You told me. You crash landed. Everything happened after…" Suspicion replaced the anxiety on her face, followed quickly by comprehension and dismay. "Oh my God." She yanked her hands away. "It was all one of your damn tricks, wasn't it?" When he didn't reply immediately, she shook her head. "God. Really? I don't know if I should be impressed or pissed off."

"I did it for you, Rachel." He'd prepared himself for anger, shock or even disappointment, but he couldn't quite face the look of horror in her eyes. "I needed to help you, but you were going to leave. And don't tell me you weren't trying to end it all. I know. I recognized the signs."

"From Nora!" She held out her hands, but withdrew them before he could take them. "I'm not Nora, Logan! You can't save her anymore." Shaking her head, she reached for her t-shirt and jeans, yanking them on. "I was perfectly happy with my deteriorating life until you came along. Trying to convince me I still have something to offer!"

"I don't think you would have come here—to me—if you were perfectly happy, Rachel." He stood, making no effort to cover himself. He caught hold of her arms, turning her to face him. "You came here for help. Like it or not, you came to me for help. And that's all I've tried to do."

Something flickered in her eyes and he had a moment of hope, but then she shook her head. "I don't know why I came here. Maybe because I'd always had a crush on you. Maybe I was looking for some sort of magic. Not this, though. Not to be tricked and fooled and played with." She snorted an ugly laugh. "Joke's on you, though, Ian Logan. Must've cost you a pretty penny to get me into bed." Her smile had turned sad. "And you coulda had me for free."

He took a step back, feeling a pain in his chest. He loved her, but he knew he'd lost her. He retreated to the truth, his hands falling to his sides. "Last night was about letting go of the past. It was about living again. And it was about the fact that I'm in love with you."

She had turned away, but his words brought her up short. She shook her head without looking back. "You should have let me go." Her voice sounded very sad. "Because whatever you think you feel for me, I'll never be able to let go of the past. And that's just the way it is."

He watched her leave, nothing left to hide. A magician without any tricks was just a man, and that was all he had to offer her in the end.

Chapter 11

He arranged for her to leave the island that afternoon. She didn't want to go with Angel, so he called in a private charter for her. He sat in his office alone, an untouched glass of Scotch on the desk next to his hand. He knew the moment her plane took off because Tammy came to stand in the door, her arms folded over her chest and a frown on her face.

"What?" He glared at her.

"What what? Did I say anything?" She glared back.

"You didn't have to." He picked up the glass and studied the drink with no real interest. "I heard it loud and clear."

"Great. Then you know I think you're an idiot. First you fall for a woman who is actively trying to destroy herself. You risk your reputation, your fortune and even your freedom to help her repair herself and then you just stand back and watch her leave? Aren't you going to at least go after her?"

"Why?" He shrugged, setting the drink aside and folding his arms on the desk in front of him. He fixed Tammy with an attentive look, a student in front of a teacher. "Why would I?"

She threw her hands to the ceiling in a gesture of frustration. "God! To protect your investment if nothing else!"

"There's no need." He stood, heading to the window. On an afterthought, he turned back and picked up the glass. "I did it. She can move on with her life. But she doesn't want me in it. Now go away, Tammy. I want to get drunk." He tipped the glass back and drank half its contents in one gulp.

Tammy made a sound of disgust, but he sensed her presence leave the room. Outside, he could see the pool and the beach beyond. The DJ was playing the music too loud. He should check into having the bar turn it back a little, but he felt listless, his energy spent. Maybe he'd go back to the island to re-energize. He was always happier there.

He wondered where Tony and Andre were. They'd apologized. Sabrina, too, just before she and her crew left. Not that they really had any reason to apologize. Evidently the storm was worse than he'd thought. He should have paid more attention, checked in at first light, made sure they knew he was fine. But when they couldn't get in touch with him, they'd had no choice but to come to his rescue. Want it or not.

And a few more hours wouldn't have made much difference anyway. He might have been able to tell Rachel in his own time, but it wouldn't have made any difference in the end. She'd rounded the corner of her grief with him, but that was fated to be as far as they'd go together. At least he knew she would survive it, even if it was alone for now.

****

Rachel stood in the middle of the dark living room, searching for some connection, some sense of belonging. God, had she actually lived in this place? She'd decorated and furnished this house. It had been a home to her. She knew it, but she didn't feel it now. It looked familiar, but only as if she'd seen pictures in a magazine or book. Maybe a movie.

On the other hand, she could close her eyes and sense the song of the jungle resonating in her heart. She could feel the muggy warmth of the air like a blanket on her skin. Even now. A thousand miles away in a different, air-conditioned lifetime and still it haunted her. She dreamed of it when she slept.

When she dreamed of Logan.

Anger lanced her at his name. Her eyes snapped open. No, she wouldn't dream of him. Never again. Not even in her dreams would she give him such pleasure.

The anger gave her the energy she needed. She hauled her luggage upstairs and unpacked, dropping her laundry down the chute. She paused, her hand on the red bikini. Jesus.

She'd worn that, used her body to escape her reality, seduced men she barely knew... She remembered the Spanish kid whose name she still didn't know, but her mind skittered away from that. She wasn't ready to face the dark things she'd done. She was only ready to face what needed to be done now.

****

Two weeks later, Rachel surveyed her living room again. Strangely, it seemed more familiar to her now than it had when she'd come home. Strange because now all the photos and mementos were gone, packed away in storage. The room was a blank slate with no hint of another life having been lived there. It might have been a display for a model home.

How much better could it all have turned out if the people involved had been different. If she and Kevin had cried and mourned and healed together. If Angel had withstood temptation and been a true sister. If Rachel herself had been stronger in the face of adversity.

She'd kept to herself in these two weeks. She'd packed and shipped and rearranged and ordered out a lot. She'd stayed away from old friends and acquaintances, avoided spots where she might run into someone she knew. She had resolutely kept her mind away from Logan and the Spanish kid and Logan and the island...and Logan...

But now, faced with the moment when the doorbell would ring and her old life would come crashing down—or at least inching in—on her, she sought her memories of her "other" life. Who here would believe the things she'd done? What would they say? The realization that they would be completely shocked was oddly freeing. She'd done everything they could imagine, so what more was there to talk about?

And Logan. She missed him with a longing that seemed almost like the pit in her soul that her baby's loss had created. The one Logan had helped her to heal, or at least begin the healing process. But this pit was in her heart and there was no way anyone but him could heal it. And she couldn't allow that.

The doorbell rang and she jerked to attention, nervous again. What was the name of the agent? Dottie. Tall, blonde, loud. Kevin had suggested her when Rachel told him she wanted to sell the house and split the money. The house was in her name now, spoils of the divorce, but it didn't feel right anymore. She didn't need it, and she no longer cared enough to continue torturing Kevin.

Dottie. Rachel reminded herself again as she opened the door, spilling light on the interior of the house.

But it wasn't Dottie. It was Angel, blinking in the sunshine. Rachel looked at her younger sister, dumbfounded, uncertain how to react to the unexpected onslaught of her past in the face of the one person she felt most betrayed by. But none of the past mattered anyway, did it? Her former disgust and anger gave way to a sense of relief accompanied by something a little sweeter that she didn't want to face just yet.

"I didn't want to be married to him anymore anyway."

She didn't realize she'd spoken the words out loud until Angel gave her a startled look. "Pardon?"

Rachel flashed her a quick—and for the first time in a long while—genuine smile. "Sorry. Kevin. I didn't want to be married to him anymore. So what you did doesn't really matter."

Angel frowned. "Jesus, Rachel. I came here to make sure you were okay and you insult me first thing?"

Rachel threw back her head and laughed. It felt good to laugh and it felt even better not to worry about what her sister would think. "I'm not trying to insult you, sis. It was just something I realized. I don't resent you anymore. I forgive you. In fact, I'm not sure I need to forgive you. You didn't take anything from me. I was done with him anyway."

Angel opened her mouth and closed it again. Then she said in a very small voice, "You make Kevin sound like a toy or a blouse or something."

"Maybe." Rachel shrugged, turning and going back into the house without closing the door. Let that be her sister's invitation to follow.

Evidently it was enough. Angel followed, looking around the house as they passed from the foyer through the living room and into the kitchen. "I like what you've done with the place."

"I'm sure you do." Rachel searched her fridge and came up with two bottles of green tea. She set one in front of her sister and uncapped the other. "The sooner I sell it, the sooner you guys can get your own place, right?"

Angel hesitated, then shrugged. "You seem to be into the whole brutally honest thing now, so yeah. That's about right."

"Good. I'll do everything I can." Rachel turned away, searching the cabinets this time. She found a package of Oreos and held it up with a questioning look. At Angel's nod, she placed the package between them and opened it.

Angel twisted the top off her cookie and licked the creamy inside out. "Why the change of heart, though? I thought you'd never forgive us for what we did." Her gaze didn't quite meet her sister's.

She doesn't think I should forgive her. Rachel bit into her cookie and chewed. She'd never been one to dissect her food and couldn't understand Angel's inability to eat an Oreo whole. "I told you, I'm not sure there's anything to forgive anymore. My marriage wasn't real. I'm not sure it ever was, but it definitely wasn't by the time you and Kevin…"

She took another bite of the cookie, only to find it stuck in her throat. She choked and reached for her tea. She lowered her gaze to the counter, concentrated on chewing and swallowing, no longer certain the words she said were true. She'd thought about them, wondered how it would feel to say them, and now that she was confronted by her sister, words just didn't have the meaning she wanted them to have.

A memory came to her of playing Barbie dolls with Angel when they were kids. She took another sip of tea, trying to swallow the lump in her throat and realized abruptly that it had nothing to do with cookies. What she was choking on was the fear of losing the girl she'd loved in her resentment of the woman.

"Rachel?" For once, the concern in Angel's voice didn't grate on Rachel's nerves. "Are you okay?"

For answer, Rachel shook her head, raising her gaze to meet her sister's, tears flowing down her cheeks now, the sob in her throat too much to swallow anymore. "Oh honey." Angel rounded the counter, catching her sister in her arms. So much had passed between them, Rachel almost didn't expect to fit in her sister's embrace anymore, but miraculously she did and she leaned into the comfort of it with gratitude.

It felt good to let go. Tears, sobs, all the emotions she'd denied herself when the baby died. She cried for the baby, for Angel, for herself and even the Spanish kid. And for Logan. And Angel held on through the storm. Rachel finally pulled away, kissed her sister's cheek and went to the bathroom for a tissue. She looked at her face in the mirror and groaned. The real estate agent might be there at any moment and she was a total mess. She washed her face, deciding it didn't matter if she met the woman without makeup on.

Angel had resumed her seat on the barstool. She glanced over her shoulder. "I texted Dottie. Told her to give us half an hour." She smiled a little, insecure smile. Tenuous but hopeful over the distance between them. "It's not much time."

Rachel nodded. Not much time, so say what you need to say. And don't waste this opportunity. "When the baby died...something in me died, too. I don't know exactly what happened but I wasn't me anymore. I'd put everything—every hope and dream I'd ever had—into that pregnancy. And when I failed at it, it...just didn't seem to matter any more. Nothing mattered. You and Kevin and my friends...I just couldn't be here. And then you guys—"

"We never meant to hurt you." Angel's face turned red. "I don't even know how it happened. We couldn't get through to you and we both hurt and it was like it was the only way..." She couldn't seem to meet Rachel's gaze. "I'm so sorry, Rachel. I love you so much."

"And now you love Kevin."

Silence fell between them and then Rachel took the last few steps across the kitchen and sat next to Angel at the bar. She placed both her hands palms down on the countertop and looked at them. "I've done a lot of things since I left, Angel. Some ugly things." She thought of doing tai chi with Logan and smiled. "Some beautiful." She turned to face her sister. "None of them are things I ever thought I was capable of when I lived in this house. So I'm not going to say that all that happened doesn't matter, because it does. And I'm not going to say that it's forgotten, because it's not. But I do want to move on with my life, and I still want you in it."

"Thank you." Angel whispered the words, her eyes bright with tears. She reached over to give Rachel an awkward sideways hug and they held on for several seconds. When they released each other, Angel cleared her throat. "And how about Logan?"

"Logan." Rachel's heart thumped oddly at the sound of his name. It was the first time she'd spoken it since she left the island. She wondered if he had said her name since she left...and abruptly she wanted nothing more than to hear him say it like he had that night, breathless and loving, whispered in her ear... She shook off the thought and stood. "Logan has nothing to do with this."

"If it weren't for Logan, where would you be?" Angel caught her arm and when Rachel gave her a querying look, she added, "I know why he did it. He knew you were trying to destroy yourself. I don't think he wanted to admit he was falling in love with you at first."

"In love?" Rachel shook her head, summoning her obstinate nature. "Deception doesn't seem like love to me."

"He put your needs before his own. He risked everything for you, Rachel. And you can't tell me we'd be sitting here having this conversation if he hadn't done what he did."

"Drugged me, faked a plane crash, kidnapped me and held me hostage?" Rachel raised her eyebrows. "He's lucky I didn't call the police."

"I thought it was a little extreme, too." Angel primmed up her lips and caught her sister's eye, then they both dissolved into laughter. Angel stood and put her arms around Rachel, clinging to her for a long moment. When she finally drew back, her eyes were full of tears and her voice hitched a little. "Sweetie, I'm not even sure you'd be here if it weren't for Logan. He saw something in you that I'd missed. Tell me you weren't thinking of suicide and I'll shut up. But if you were, then I think you have to start thanking Logan for his intervention."

Intervention. Rachel remembered the longing to let the blackness take her and shivered a little. How close had she come? I believe in fate in as far as I believe we are fated to reach certain points in our lives where we have to make decisions. But I believe the decisions we make are our own. Had Logan's actions helped her avoid a fate she really didn't want?

****

April in the North Carolina mountains was always unpredictable weather-wise, Logan thought. He much preferred the Caribbean where he could count on weather warm enough for him to wear t-shirts and shorts. But he'd come straight from the airport to his mother-in-law's house, and now he sat, sweltering, in a dark suit on the patio while Jasmine played happily on the swings and Celia, his mother-in-law, did her best to make him feel comfortable with iced tea and a plate of cookies.

Not that the warm sun really mattered in the face of his daughter's joy at seeing him. For the first time ever, when she flung her arms around his neck, he let himself bask in her affection, hugging her back with a return of affection he finally felt free to express.

And I owe that to Rachel. He'd never expected to find his own peace while trying to help her, but he had. In spite of the sleepless nights he'd spent without her, she'd healed something inside him that he hadn't even realized was broken. If nothing else, their short-lived relationship had helped them both deal with their losses.

"You're different."

He looked up in surprise, smiling a little into his mother-in-law's bright eyes. Celia, like her daughter, was very straightforward, almost in a childlike way. It had its charm as well as its annoyances. He raised his eyebrows, "How do you mean?"

"You're...not exactly happy, but like you could be." She nodded with satisfaction. "That's good."

At one time, he never would have believed this woman would be satisfied he could be happy, but now he wondered if she'd ever really blamed him for Nora's death. Maybe his own perception of his guilt had overwhelmed all other considerations.

He sipped his tea and loosened his tie. "Bit of a heatwave isn't it? Aren't you still supposed to be able to ski around here?"

"Ski season ends in March for good reason. You can't depend on the weather to be cold." Celia looked out over the mountains that made up her back yard. "It's spring now. Time for the flowers to wake up."

"That's what Nora always used to say." Her name escaped him before he thought, but she didn't flinch.

"I used to tell her that when she was Jasmine's age." Celia heaved a long sigh. "It's almost time for something else, isn't it? For Jasmine to go home with you?"

The wistfulness in her voice made his heart ache. He reached for her hand. "I would never want to take her from you."

"I know that." Celia nodded. "You could have done it a long time ago if you wanted to. But the fact is your seasons are changing. You can offer her something I can't now. A real parent."

"You've been a parent in every way that's really important." He stopped when she pulled her hand away.

She didn't speak immediately, but when she did, he knew she'd considered every word carefully. "I know why you wanted me to take care of her for you. I know your guilt weighed you down for a long time. And I let you feel that way so I could have Jasmine to help me heal." She looked at her hands folded in front of her for a moment, then back at him. "That's something I'll live with."

"If having Jasmine helped you in any way with Nora's loss, I'm grateful." He tried to put his sincerity into his voice.

She nodded and they were silent for several seconds before she spoke again. "It doesn't change the fact that it's time for both of us to get on with the lives we were meant to lead. You as a father, me as a grandmother."

He hesitated, wanting to confirm her words but not sure how. Though he hadn't taken the time to plan it out, he'd known he needed to broach the subject with her. He watched his daughter playing quietly in the little playhouse someone else had built for her. "She should finish the school year here."

"Her spring break is next week." Celia considered. "I wouldn't mind spending it on a warm beach." She paused, giving him an impish smile that reminded him again of Nora. "Summer break too, for that matter."

"There are worse places to retire than tropical islands." He grinned.

"Daddy!" The enthusiastic shout caught his attention and his heart, turning him to meet his daughter as she sprang into his arms. "Daddy, Grammie says the ice cream shop is open again. Can we go?"

He buried his face in his daughter's lilac-scented blonde hair. These childish requests for instant gratification would come more and more often if he were going to be a real father to his daughter. He kissed her forehead and then said, "How about this deal? You eat all your broccoli at dinner and we get ice cream for dessert? My treat."

She played with his tie, settling into his lap and looking up at him with big brown eyes and a serious, measuring expression he'd felt on his own face at times. "You mean you're staying for dinner?"

"Yes. I do mean that." He hugged her, thinking of the other flying visits he'd paid his daughter. An hour or two here and there, unable to hold her for longer because he'd been so caught up in the guilt and shame. But none of that had anything at all to do with the beautiful little girl in his arms. "In fact, how about I stay for a few days and take you and Grammie back to the island with me?"

Her eyes widened. "You mean it? For real? I've got a passport. Grammie showed me and said when I was big enough I'd go back to your island with you. Am I really big enough?"

Celia reached across the table to squeeze his hand and only then did he realize his vision had blurred with tears. He hugged Jasmine harder, grateful he'd finally cleared the guilt from his heart, leaving plenty of room for love. "Yeah, sweetie. You're really big enough. Finally."

****

Rachel stepped out of the real estate office, feeling free for the first time in years. It was more than just selling the house she'd bought with Kevin. It was a release of negative emotions she no longer wished to be bound to. She wanted to fling her arms wide to the sky and dance and sing.

This is what Logan was talking about. She took a deep breath and turned as Kevin and Angel exited the office together. Kevin gave her the cautious look he'd taken to using around her. As if he didn't really know her, had no idea what her next action would be. And maybe he hadn't. Maybe that was what had happened to them. She only knew that right now, six months after her return home, more than a year since her divorce and almost two since her baby died...now she was ready to get on with her life. Although how she could do that, she didn't know.

One foot in front of the other. And I might as well start out right. She held out her hand to Kevin. "I guess this is it."

And it was. With the house sold, there was nothing else to bind them. Standing there on the sunny street in the small North Carolina town, there was nothing left of the five years they'd been together. It was as clean a break as she could manage anymore.

He took her hand, still with a wary look in his eye. "I guess so. See you around, huh?"

"Maybe."

"Rachel, don't be mysterious." Angel sounded not wary but half panicked. "The last time you did that you disappeared for a month."

Rachel hugged her sister. "I have no intention of disappearing again. I just don't, honestly, know what I'm going to do now. Or where I'm going to go." She backed away from Angel, careful to keep hold of her hands long enough to give them a reassuring squeeze. "It's not a bad thing, though. I have my life to live and discover. Whatever's waiting for me, I finally feel ready for it."

She held her sister's gaze for just a moment more. She knew her words were meant as much to reassure herself as her sister. She'd never been so adrift in the world before without a safety line of family or job or home. And as exciting as a new beginning might sound, it also unsettled and threatened. But if she believed it included dancing and singing, maybe it just would.

****

Jasmine, wrapped in a towel and sitting on her grandmother's lap in the warm sun, watched the salt shaker with all her might as Logan covered it with a napkin. His heart filled with delight at her scrutiny. She was always trying to figure out how he "did it", but she never ceased to be amazed by a new trick. Her persistence drove him to try harder and harder sleight of hand, exercising muscles he'd thought long atrophied from disuse.

Now, as she watched, he moved the napkin-covered shaker over the solid table by the side of the pool. "I'm pretty sure there's a soft spot here somewhere." He pretended to search, then jerked back as if in surprise, releasing the napkin to fall flat on the table.

Jasmine squealed with happy surprise. "Where'd the shaker go?"

He produced it from under the table, grinning at her applause, but a little surprised when it was echoed from not only Andre and Stacey, who were also seated with them, but also by a small crowd of onlookers. He gave a half-bow. "Thank you. I'm here all week."

Laughter and the other guests politely dissipated, leaving him alone with his friends and family. Celia looked relaxed, Logan was happy to note. When they'd first come to the island that summer, she'd mentioned going home when Jasmine was settled into school, but here she was, four months later, obviously content. It worked well for Jazz, who loved her grandmother very much. Although, he was proud to admit, she hadn't had much trouble adjusting to life with him as the primary caregiver, either.

"You know, you could be." Stacey adjusted the pink-wrapped bundle in her lap, a gentle smile on her face. Motherhood had smoothed what harsh edges had been left in her soul, leaving her almost completely happy in her love for her husband and child.

Logan was glad they'd brought the baby with them on this trip. It was good to see her this way and his old friend so content in his family. Distracted by these happy thoughts, it took him a moment to process what Stacey had just said. Then he frowned. "What? Wait a sec—"

Andre held up a hand, interrupting without apology. "She's right, you know. You were one of the best, Logan. Magic still needs you."

Jasmine listened to the adult interchange, then slipped from her grandmother's lap and rounded the table to stand in front of her father, still holding the salt. "You're a magician." She nodded. "One of my friends at school said you were, but I wasn't sure I knew exactly what she was saying right."

"I was a magician." Logan kissed his daughter's forehead. "But that was a long time ago. Before you were born."

Jasmine handed him the salt shaker. "You still are." She grinned at him cheerfully and skipped over to the playground.

Celia stood to follow her granddaughter, but paused to look at Logan. "If you don't mind my two-cents, I think Nora would want you to go back to what you loved. She knew how happy performing magic made you—and how happy it made other people. I don't think she'd want to see you give it up."

"Why don't you give it a try? Just on a trial basis." Stacey leaned carefully over the baby to sip her lemonade. "Umm. That's really good. But seriously, you've got an outside theater, don't you? For concerts and things? Just do it here, among friends."

"You might want to let the media know about it." Andre considered. "I'll call Tony. He'll make sure the right people know. It'll be good publicity for the resort."

Logan raised his eyebrows and sipped his own drink. *You still are.* His daughter was right, really. He was still a magician. It wasn't something you could just stop being like an accountant. It was an integral part of who he was, so even if he didn't practice magic, he was still a magician.

Making a decision, he set aside his drink. "Okay, let's do it. But let's do it right."

****

Andre looked around at the little library curiously. It honestly didn't seem a likely place to find the exotic beauty his best friend had fallen in love with, but he had good reason to know that people didn't always end up in the place they first set a course to. And Angel, who had been happier to see him than he'd anticipated, had assured him Rachel worked here now.

He scanned the library one last time and his gaze fell on the reference desk off to the side with the laminated sign that read, "Got Questions?" A woman was busy at the computer behind the desk. He shrugged. Better place to start than any. As he approached, the woman at the desk looked up, her dark hair falling back from her face. They both froze.

"Andre?" Rachel frowned and stood. "What are you doing here?"

Did her voice contain just a little hope? If so, it would indicate forgiveness and that could make his job that much easier. He proceeded with caution. "Sometimes I'm reminded of how small a world we live in. I was visiting my mother. I grew up in Bath."

She smiled, a warm smile very unlike the sexy but brittle one he remembered, and for the first time he got a glimpse of what Logan had known was there all along. "That's such a beautiful little town," she said. "I've been there a couple of times, just to visit."

"Not much other reason to go there if you don't have family." He made a conscious effort to stop himself from nodding like an idiot. God, she was downright charming. For the first time since meeting her, he could really see why Logan had fallen for her. All the pretense was gone, and what it left behind—in a ponytail and almost no makeup—was extraordinary.

Only when she laughed a little did he realize he was staring. He grinned. "I'm—very sorry. I just—almost wouldn't recognize you. You seem much happier."

Her laughter died, but she nodded, her face sober. "I am happier. In a lot of ways."

The ruefulness of her tone gave him hope again. "He misses you too." When she looked doubtful, he added. "Logan.

He does. I swear. But he won't call you if you're waiting for that."

"I'm not." She stated it simply and sat back down at the reference desk. "Did you need anything else?"

"You're as stubborn as he is, aren't you?" He shook his head. "Both of you in love and pining away for each other, but you won't admit it."

"Pining away?" She looked up at him, amused. "I wouldn't exactly call it pining away. Wasting away...but never pining."

He laughed and shrugged. "Well, whatever you want to call it, you miss him."

"I do." She looked at her hands, then spread them wide, palms up, a gesture of helplessness. "But what do I do? If there's one thing life's taught me, it's that sometimes what's done is done."

"What's done is done, but what's to come isn't." He squatted in front of her desk, looking into her eyes earnestly. "Come back to the island. I'll make all the arrangements. Show him you're willing to take the first step in deciding your own fate." He paused. "He's planning a show. For his daughter's sake, I think. She said she wanted to see him perform."

"Jasmine?" An odd shadow passed over her face. Then she nodded. "So he's taken her back to live with him. That's good. She needs him."

"And he needs her. But that's not all he needs."

"I can see how you became famous as the master of illusion." She picked up a book, set it down again and removed her glasses. She fixed him with her steady glare, as disarming suddenly as it had been the first time he met her. "What you're ignoring here are the things he and I have already done. And I'm not sure I can ever be the person he wants me to be."

He sighed, placing both hands on the desk in front of her, deliberately adopting an attitude of defeat. "Okay. Yeah. I'm the last person to tell you two people who love each other can't hurt each other. A lot more than two people who really don't like each other, actually. And our actions are very, very hard to overcome. But if we try..." He straightened, spread his hands and produced a rose. "It's the equivalent of magic."

"You guys just can't help yourselves, can you?" She took the rose he offered and twirled it between her fingers. "How's your wife, by the way?"

"Happy. With an eight pound bundle of pink-garbed joy. Are you going to take me up on my offer?"

"Maybe." She appeared lost in thought.

"Maybe?" He raised his eyebrows.

Her gaze snapped back to his. "Maybe. It's the best I can do right now. Make the arrangements and send me the details. If you're willing to do that, maybe I'll be there."

He nodded, knowing when he'd been bested. "Fine. But know that his night won't be complete without you in it. And his life won't either."

Her only reply was a slightly sideways smile. "That's not really my problem, is it?"

****

Not really my problem. Right. She sat alone in the hotel room overlooking the twilit river. A few boats still moved across the wide expanse, their lights like fireflies from this distance.

The room wasn't exactly lavish, but it was comfortable. All she needed. And all she had at that point. She certainly had the ability to provide herself with a more permanent situation, but for some reason she hadn't been able to follow through on any inviting prospects.

I'm working part time as a library assistant in a town I no longer feel at home in and I'm staying at a hotel. She sipped her hot tea and looked out at the water. Her life felt as fluid and in motion as the river. She couldn't seem to get a handle on it anymore. She shifted her gaze to the sky and spotted a star. With her left hand, she felt in her pocket, pulled out the little velvet bag she kept what she thought of as her "star crystal" out. Did you see a trick?

No. She hadn't seen the trick then or when he trapped her in a "crash landing." But there had been one. Because magic didn't exist. It was all tricks and sleight of hand.

But was it? She shook the crystal into her hand and closed her fingers over it as she remembered the jungle. The primal magic there had been palpable, as real as the crystal in her hand, and he had been as eager to share that with her as he had the trick of catching the star. Maybe more so. Because he'd cared what happened to her.

His night won't be complete without you in it. And his life won't either. But was that true? Really? He didn't even know her. He knew the her from ten years ago. He knew the her from six months ago. But he didn't know her because she wasn't even sure she knew herself. And what if what she was wasn't enough? Or too much?

She stood, shaking her head. No. She wasn't going to do this again. Not again. She was just starting to discover herself. Or at least, who she could be. Not Kevin's wife, not the half-crazed divorcee, not even the innocent young woman who'd once been so in awe of her best friend's famous husband she'd shied away from any situations which put them in close contact. Right now she was in limbo. Living in a hotel room because she couldn't make up her mind to stay here. But she had started her journey to finding herself and she couldn't allow the fear that what she found wouldn't be what someone else wanted to hold her back.

Maybe I started it back on the island. In his arms. The thought made her pause. She looked down at the crystal in her hand, then back up, a little startled at the sight of her own reflection in the darkening hotel window. That's me.

She walked to the window, staring at the reflection as she got closer. Slender but strong. I've been through enough. I should be strong. She tilted her head and looked more critically. Her left eye was slightly larger than her right. But that was okay because her right breast was slightly larger than her left. She smiled at the thought and noticed how her lips rose higher on one side than the other. She was starting—just barely—to get laugh lines around her eyes. I'm getting older.

She remembered her mother saying something when she was young. As you get older, your time gets shorter. For the first time, really, she began to grasp what her mother had meant. She looked at her reflection for a moment longer. She felt strangely as if she were seeing an old friend again for the first time in a long time. But that's just me. And I've been here all along.

Absurdly the words Logan had said to her after the "plane crash" came back to her. I like the world better with you in it.

She touched her reflection and smiled a little. "Maybe he actually had something there."

Chapter 12

Rachel stepped off the plane half expecting Andre to be there to meet her, half dreading that he might have sent Logan. But neither of the handsome magicians waited in the little island terminal. Instead, an older woman dressed in a relaxed hot pink blouse and neat white pants stood from one of the pastel colored rocking chairs that lined the room. "Rachel?"

"Celia?" Rachel gaped at the older woman, then half ran to her. Celia enveloped her in the type of embrace only a mother could give. "Oh my God, it's so good to see you."

"I asked Andre if I could meet the plane on the off-chance that you came." Celia backed away, holding her at arm's length and smiling at her, a few tears in her eyes. "I've missed you." She stroked a lock of Rachel's hair, clearing her throat. "You stopped coming to visit."

"I know." Rachel remembered the last time she'd visited. Jasmine had only been a couple of years old, just starting to toddle around, and she'd told Celia about being engaged to Kevin. God, had it really been that long? Overcome by remorse, she hugged Celia hard. "I'm so sorry."

The older woman patted her back, then took her hand and led her to the baggage area. "Let's get your bags and I'll take you to your room. We have a lot of catching up to do."

Rachel spent the short ride to the hotel in silence, but she held Celia's hand and thought about all this woman had given her over the years. Her own mother, who now lived in Florida, had always been a remote woman, more concerned with social standing and her career than with childcare. Rachel and Angel had taken care of each other a lot, but Rachel had also had Celia to go to in her teenage years. Nora had never balked at sharing her mother, and Celia's warm personality had been more than enough to get both girls through first dates and the difficult days of being a new driver and the many other social crises girls go through in high school and college, especially in a small town.

Oh, Nora. What would you think of me now? What would you think of the things I've done? And the things your husband had to stop me from doing. She shuddered in remembered horror. She'd come so close.

Celia squeezed her hand. "We're here."

They'd given her the same suite she'd stayed in before. How exactly had they managed it? Andre wouldn't have told Logan she was coming, and she was fairly certain he had no idea she was there now. If he had, he would have been at the airport.

So now what?

She turned to Celia. "Is Jasmine here?"

Celia nodded. "I'd love to reintroduce you." She paused, then hurried on, as if eager to say what she needed to before she lost courage. "Ian told me. About you two."

"Ian?" Rachel smiled a little. "I thought everyone had stopped calling him that."

The older woman sniffed. "He tried to get me to stop, but I ignored him."

"Yeah, that makes sense." Rachel ran her fingers across the dustless surface of the desk. "I hope...I hope you don't think I..." What could she say? How could she finish that sentence? I hope you don't think I'm betraying Nora? I hope you don't think I'm disrespecting the memory of the best friend I've ever had? What did it matter at this point when her sins were so much more numerous and damaging?

Her friend's mother understood, however. She sat on the couch. "You know, you always fit into our family so easily. Seamlessly. As if you and Nora were actually meant to be sisters instead of best friends." Her expression was rueful. "Once or twice, I actually wished you were." She laughed. "Who am I kidding? Nora wasn't an only child, but she and her sister never really got along, and she was such a tender soul. You made her so happy, whenever you were around. I loved it. I loved you." She reached for Rachel's hand and squeezed. "I love you, and I love Ian and if you two can make each other happy, I'm all for it."

Rachel wondered if they could or if she and Logan weren't really meant to be. But that was what she was here to find out, and having the approval of the one woman who still bound her life to Logan's meant a lot. She squeezed Celia's hand and searched for a reply that would express some of the fullness in her heart. Before she could find it, however, the door flew open and a little girl came bounding in. "Gramma! I went swimming with Uncle Andre and we found live sea stars!"

Jasmine. Rachel's heart gave an unexpected leap at the sight of the little girl, who reminded her so much of her old friend she couldn't possibly have been anyone else's daughter. She was so tall. Dear God. How had so much time passed?

Celia cleared her throat and turned. "Have you forgotten all your manners, young lady? How do you enter a room where two adults are talking?"

"Oh." The tiny cutie with the curly dark hair like her mother's and the dark eyes like her father's stopped and looked shyly at Rachel. "Sorry. I shouldn't have interrupted. It was very rude."

Rachel couldn't help but smile at the little girl's articulate apology. "That's okay, sweetheart. You were excited, huh?"

Jasmine's face lit up. "Yes! It was awesome! Gramma, can you come next time, please?"

"Snorkeling? I don't think so." Celia shot Rachel a sly look. "But maybe Miss Rachel would like to join you and your father sometime."

"Oh, could you?" Jasmine grabbed Rachel's hands with the confidence of a bright child. "We would have so much fun."

Uncertain how to react to such an unexpected turn of events, Rachel cleared her throat and glanced at Celia.

"Jasmine, there'll be time for that later," Celia smiled and kissed the little girl's head. "But I'm glad you're here. Miss Rachel was a friend of your mother's."

"You knew my mommy?" Jasmine's face illuminated even more, if that was possible. "Can you tell me about her? Gramma tells me stories and we write her letters sometimes."

Sudden tears threatened and Rachel had an almost overwhelming urge to sweep the little girl into an embrace, but she blinked rapidly and bit her lip, smiling at the innocent request. "Of course. I loved your mommy a lot and I would like to tell you all about her. I met you before, you know. A long time ago."

"When I was a baby?"

"Yeah." Rachel remembered the beautiful pink-wrapped bundle she'd held during the funeral. How had she let it go so long without visiting Jasmine and Celia? She could have been a part of this child's life all along. But the pain and guilt of her friend's death had been so fresh back then, and distance had selfishly allowed her to dull her own pain while leaving her friend's family—her family—to go on without her.

Celia put her hand on Jasmine's head and caught Rachel's eye. The depth of understanding in her gaze surprised Rachel. "We should let you rest and get ready."

"Oh, are you coming to the magic show?" Jasmine clapped her hands. "Oh goody. Do you know my daddy, too?"

"Yes." Rachel choked a little on the word. "Yes, I do. And yes, I'm looking forward to the magic show."

"Will you sit with us? We're sitting right up front." Jasmine turned to her grandmother. "She can, can't she?"

"Wouldn't have it any other way." Celia kissed Rachel on the cheek and looked her in the eye. "I'm sure it will make your father very happy to see her there."

****

"I really hope we're doing the right thing." Lydia's mutter was just audible as she and Stacey walked around the pool toward the table where Celia, Jasmine, Tony and Andre clustered around Logan.

"Do you really have any doubts?" Stacey gave Lydia a sharp look. Andre's love had brightened her own horizons so significantly she only wanted to share that view with everyone else, but Lydia's sharp edge sometimes made that difficult. "Don't you think they deserve a chance to be happy?"

Lydia laughed. "I don't mean that I don't want Logan to be happy or that I doubt his judgment in any way. Of anyone or anything. So stop being all protective mama on me and save it for your daughter." She put her arm around Stacey's shoulders and gave her a hug. "I just wonder if Ian is really ready for this."

Stacey blinked a little at Lydia's use of Logan's first name. Of course, he'd only used his last name for as long as she'd know him, but Lydia had been his friend before. In happier times. "You mean the magic show, not Rachel."

Lydia widened her green eyes a little and nodded. "Yeah. That's what I mean. Magic—at least at Ian Logan's level—well, it's not like doing a birthday party for kids. It's a commitment, even an addiction. Maybe more than love, even, when you think of the practice and the secrets and the overall—" She swept her arms wide with a helpless gesture and then laughed a little. "Well, commitment. That's it. And I know you know. You're married to one of the best magicians I know."

"I am." Stacey watched as Andre started toward them. He had not expressed any concern about the show and Logan's readiness for it. But he also hadn't started calling Logan by his first name, either. She considered for a moment the possibility that a woman in the same field might have a different— perhaps more accurate—take on Logan's readiness to return to performing.

Before she could allow any further doubts to enter her mind, however, Andre met them and she summoned her most confident smile. "Hey, what did you do with our daughter?"

"She's bonding with her Uncle Tony." Andre kissed his wife. "I think he mentioned needing to get one for himself."

"Oh God, don't start putting ideas in his head already." Lydia rolled her eyes and continued around the pool.

Andre chuckled. "She can say what she likes, but I'm betting a family isn't too far from her mind, either." He turned back to his wife. "Everything set?"

"Well, she's here." Stacey slipped her arm around her husband and they continued around the pool at a slower pace than Lydia. "Celia said she's sure Rachel wants to see him, too. And she bribed Jasmine to keep the secret."

Andre pulled her a little closer. "Are you sure this is a good idea?"

"Of course it's a good idea." She gave him a quelling look. Now was no time for doubts. "He's in love with her, right?"

"And she walked out on him."

"If memory serves, I walked out on you in the beginning. Didn't slow you down much."

"I think that was more of a mutual walking out." He considered. "But yeah. I didn't hesitate to try to get you back once I'd come to my senses."

"Well then, we need to make sure he gets the same chance. And he'll never do it on his own. He thinks she has good reason to never forgive him."

"I'm sort of ambivalent about that, actually." He shrugged at her sharp look. "Well, she could have had us all arrested."

Before Stacey could protest, they were at the table and Logan rose from his seat. He plucked his daughter up and settled her on his shoulders. "Well, we should do this thing if we're gonna."

"You don't want to do it?" Stacey felt her first stab of real doubt, remembering Lydia's comments. She stepped over to him under the pretense of straightening his shirt collar.

"I didn't say that." Logan gave her a fond smile. "And I'm pretty sure my collar's not going to stay straight with a munchkin on my shoulders."

"Come on, Daddy, I want to see some magic!" Jasmine hugged her father's head.

"Do you, sweetie?" He swung her down to hug her before handing her to Celia. "Okay then. Go get your front row seat."

"Good luck," Celia smiled as she set Jasmine down and they walked across the lawn to the auditorium, the little girl blowing him kisses as they went.

"There, see?" Stacey knew she was seeking reassurance for her actions. "She wants to see you perform." She bit her lip and glanced at the others then back at him. "This is your moment, Logan. It's been six months since Rachel left and six years since Nora died. It's time. Show your baby girl what you can do."

He gave her an odd look from his depthless eyes. She said a quiet prayer that what was going through his head was a newfound determination to rebuild his career—and his life. But when he replied she couldn't really tell from his words if he meant them. "Yeah. It's time. Let's do it."

****

The little outside auditorium hummed with anticipation. Logan could feel it in his heart and bones and soul. An audience waiting to be introduced. To him, to magic. To whatever acted through him to produce magic in their eyes.

He remembered this feeling. He'd once called it his addiction. The reason he hadn't wanted to leave performing for the birth of his daughter. He'd experienced it every single time he went on stage. But it was so much more than that. He'd often sworn half the magic came from the audience and their desire to believe. If he hadn't believed it before, he would now because the energy from this group of his friends and guests was intoxicating.

And it was so easy slipping back into the persona of the magician. Performing was like putting on a well-worn cloak. He walked on stage, paused to pick a hibiscus flower from the bush beside the steps. He put it in his buttonhole, passed his hand in front of it and listened to the gasp of wonder when it changed, spreading beautiful orange wings and taking flight as a butterfly. He turned with a smile to Jasmine, wanting to see the wonder and delight in her eyes.

And froze.

Sitting next to his daughter was Rachel. She wore a simple floral sundress and when her eyes met his, he suspected most of the magic he felt in the air that night came from her. But what was she doing there? Something that had sat lifeless in his chest for the past few months, spread tiny wings and gave a tentative flutter. Hope.

He glanced surreptitiously to the side stage area where Andre and Stacey lurked. Stacey looked guilty. Of course she was. Her talk about Rachel leaving six months ago was a blind. But she'd also said something else. This is your moment, Logan.

My moment. He took a deep breath, cleared his throat and faced the audience of friendly and familiar faces. "I'd like to thank you all"—his eyes sought Rachel's—"for being here. It's been a long time since I've been on stage, and, in fact, I never thought I'd do it again. But there's a funny thing about having children you love." He smiled at Jasmine and she grinned back as the spotlight centered on her. "They can make you believe in magic."

He blew his daughter a kiss and she pretended to catch it, then, just as they'd rehearsed, she blew one back. He jerked back as if something had hit him in the face, and the audience laughed at the red lipstick mark that had appeared on his cheek. He scrubbed it away with a white handkerchief that turned into a red rose, which he knelt and presented to Jasmine who kissed him again, for real this time, on the cheek. The crowd laughed and clapped, obviously loving it. Logan chanced a look at Rachel, but her face was obscured, just out of range of the spotlight. *If you're here, maybe you believe in magic again.*

****

Rachel felt his eyes on her, but couldn't risk meeting his gaze yet. The tears she'd felt so near the surface since meeting Jasmine again still threatened. She didn't want anything to mess this evening up for Logan. *Ian.* Her heart whispered his name. She wanted to say it out loud.

I don't know if this is going to work. What if he doesn't like who I am? She honestly couldn't see beyond that particular moment, sitting in the audience, trying to stay in the shadows. She couldn't imagine the next moment when she would turn to catch his eye or the end of the show when she'd have to explain why she was there—*why am I here?*—or that night when she'd go back to her room. Alone or with him.

The sensation of not knowing what the next moment would bring, let alone the next day or the next week, was unsettling but not new. She recognized it from the moment she'd stepped outside the lawyer's office with her sister and her ex-husband. From the moment she'd spotted Andre's striking figure in the little library. And because she'd spent so many months knowing that all her life would ever hold for her was more misery and self-loathing, she recognized the blessing, for once, of not knowing.

She turned her head, ready to meet his gaze at last, but it was too late. He kissed his daughter's cheek and moved away and the spotlight was gone. But he'd seen her. He knew she was there. She sensed his awareness in every move of his body as he performed each trick. Card tricks, origami, even a couple of minor escapes. None of the grand illusions that were once his hallmark, but the audience was delighted with the close-up magic tricks and simple illusions, each one carried off flawlessly.

Only at the end of the show, however, did he pause in front of her again. He didn't look down, but she knew this one was for her and her breath caught in her throat, half dread, half anticipation swirling in her.

He perched on the single stool that was his only stage prop. "Tony, can you turn the lights down a little?" He glanced up at the sky as the lights dimmed. "The stars are bright enough, don't you think?" A rustle of anticipation went through the audience and swept over Rachel, bringing her breath from her in a gasp.

Maybe the small sound caught his ear. At any rate, he looked down at her. "I have a wish I wish to make tonight." His lips curved and he stood, coming to the edge of the stage, his eyes never leaving hers. "I hope I'm not the only one." He held his hand out to her.

For what felt like forever, she hesitated, absurdly frozen in place by her very desire to take his hand. Yes, she had a wish to wish. If she could find the courage to wish it, she could be his again. She could have all she'd ever wanted. She closed her eyes, hoping the moment wouldn't pass her by before she could overcome the lingering doubt that she was truly what he wanted.

"Miss Rachel! Go!" The little voice beside her startled her into opening her eyes. Jasmine gave her a half annoyed, half urgent push. "Daddy needs you!"

Did he? She looked back at Logan. He raised his eyebrows and she found her courage and took the first step toward what she knew was the path she really wanted to take. No matter how it ended, she wanted to give it a try.

He helped her onto the stage, his hand warm around hers. When she would have turned, a little embarrassed, toward the audience, he stopped her, bringing her around to face him. "I caught a star for you once."

She nodded, finding it hard to articulate an answer. His smile warmed her, relaxing her. "It's all okay, you know. We're just doing magic tonight." He raised his voice so the rest of the audience could hear him. "Do you remember what I told you about the star?"

She cleared her throat. She remembered so much from their time together, but it all jumbled together right then. Some things you just have to take on faith. "Ian." She gave him a pleading look, but when he just tilted his head at the sound of his name, she fought to clear her mind, to focus. "You said you can't keep a star captive forever?"

He nodded. "Yes, I did. And that is true. I also said I can only catch one. But I'm not the only one who has a wish to wish tonight, am I?" He directed the last words at the audience, who, spellbound, had watched their interchange unnoticed. A murmur of assent met his question.

Keeping hold of her hands, he turned to face the light. "Tony, can you lower the lights a little more, please?" All the lights over their heads dimmed, leaving only the stage lights shining up on them. As the tropical night moved in on the audience, he closed his eyes. "My mother used to say to save your wishes for a falling star." Releasing her hands, he raised his own skyward, then slowly brought them down. She was so focused on him, she didn't notice what had happened until the audience gasped in wonder. He opened his eyes, smiling at her as bits of glittering blue-white light floated down all around them. "Make a wish."

She shook her head, her lips trembling as she gazed at him through the ethereal light of the falling stars. She reached into her pocket and took out the star crystal, holding it out to him in the palm of her hand. "I have everything I could wish for."

And as the audience applauded, he pulled her into his arms and kissed her.

****

He didn't let go of her hand while he took his bows. As soon as he could, he pulled her off stage with him, intent on stealing a few moments alone, needing to find out why she was there and what it meant before the world and his friends closed in around him. Even that moment on stage when she'd looked him in the eye and told him she had nothing else to wish for and then kissed him...after all they'd been through, he couldn't trust even that. Not without a word of reassurance from her.

He cursed the lack of a backstage to hide in, a door to lock, even a dark corridor. Everything was open behind the outdoor amphitheater. He caught sight of the laundry room he'd provided for his guests. Conveniently situated between the pool and the guestrooms, but out of the way of both, it was hardly ever inhabited, especially at this time of night. His guests would be making their way to the bars, the pool, or back to their rooms. He tugged her hand and made a run for it, hoping they wouldn't be spotted.

He didn't feel safe until they were both inside the laundry room and he'd locked the door behind them. Only then did he release her hand and turn to face her in the semi-darkness. He shook his head, fighting the urge to touch her again. "I don't understand."

"I know." She nodded. "I don't either, totally. I didn't have any intention of ever coming back here."

"You made that very clear." He studied her, noting even in the dim light that her face had a softer quality, her voice a more gentle timber. "You're different."

"You should know. You helped me get here." She took a tentative step forward. "You changed me, helped me heal, helped me forgive myself. And once I'd forgiven myself I found I could forgive others. You were right about that."

"I'm glad." He held himself still as she reached for him, closed his eyes as her hands touched his, then moved up his arms as she stepped closer. "But why did you come back?"

"To find out—if I am who you want." She half breathed the words as if afraid to speak them out loud, so close now he could feel her breasts against his chest, her lips against his neck. She leaned her head against his shoulder and he gave in to the urge to put his hands on her waist and mold her closer to him. God she felt good. So right. Still high off his show, he imagined making love to her there in the darkness of the laundry room. But surely that was something he might have done with the Rachel who'd been on the island before. The one who'd seduced and discarded men, so lost in her own pain she didn't mind causing more. He sensed this newly healed Rachel wouldn't do those things and probably regretted what she had done.

Yet it was this Rachel who was responding to his touch with a wanton desire that matched his own, unbuttoning his shirt, running her hands over his chest and kissing his neck, nibbling his ear and pressing herself against him until he could stand it no longer and he picked her up, putting her on top of the nearest machine and shrugging off his shirt, pushing the straps of her sundress over her shoulders and reaching for her bra clasp as he claimed her mouth with a ferocious passion that surprised him.

****

To find out if I am who you want. The moment she spoke the words, she knew she had finally gained the courage she needed. She wasn't the shrinking, shy, proper woman she'd been. But she only wanted one man. Ian. The problem was, she wanted him with a ferocious desire that wouldn't allow her to wait. Here. Now. And the hell with the rest of the world.

Thank God he seemed in favor of it. She gasped as he bared her breasts to the night, bending her back over the machine he'd set her on so he could caress and lap and bring her need for him rising like a tide through her entire body. She moaned. "I want you, Ian."

He paused, looked up at her with a tender smile. "I love the way you say my name." He kissed each nipple one last time, then her belly button before looking back up at her, his hands on her waist. "I want to hear you say it again and again."

Her heartbeat quickened. "Ian—"

He shook his head. "Shh. Not yet."

As he began to work her skirt up over her hips, she was torn between a desire to help him with both her clothes and his and knowing she should be worried about what his friends and family might be thinking about their sudden disappearance. But when his fingers found the damp crotch of her panties and rubbed her through the material, her traitorous body lifted of its own accord, letting him grasp the thin material and pull it aside and away, baring her to his exploring fingers caressing her, sliding inside her slick wetness as he kissed her neck and breasts, bringing her to bucking, gasping pleasure.

"Now," he whispered, as she came. "Say it now."

"Ian!" She gasped his name. He lifted her and she wrapped her arms around his waist as he supported them against the cold metal of the dryer. She felt him slide into her and she arched her back, opening herself as fully as she could to him, trembling and clinging to him.

He groaned and moved his hands to her buttocks, supporting her and holding her still at the same time. It was a sweet torture to feel him inside her and not be able to move. He kissed her neck, pushing back her sweaty mass of hair. "It won't take me long, baby. Not yet. I just want to be inside you as long as I can."

She stayed as still as possible, breathing in the scent of his aftershave and sweat and whatever the indefinable musk was that she'd come to associate with the smell of his skin. She could feel everything from the fullness of him inside her to his breath on her neck and his arms against her sides, bracing them both against the dryer.

The desire to feel him move inside her overcame the last of her reserve, and she kissed him, nipped at his earlobe, slid her hands into his hair, and he obliged with a groan before he began to move, slow, smooth, gliding strokes that unhinged any inhibitions she might have left. She forgot they were locked inside a laundry room and he was making love to her against one of the machines. She forgot that his friends and mother-in-law and daughter were waiting for them somewhere, eager to congratulate him on his successful show and welcome her to the family. She even forgot that the last time they'd made love they'd parted on less than friendly terms.

Nothing mattered except this. The smooth strokes, the hot breath, the beads of sweat trickling off her, the heat, the passion, the feel of his skin against hers and the pleasure. Oh God, the pleasure and fulfillment of having him inside her again couldn't be wrong when it felt like this. It built in her middle with each of his strokes, and she wanted to hold back, but as he began to move faster it was impossible and she cried out his name again. And as if it were what he'd waited for, his thrusts became faster and harder and then he came with a hot rush inside her and they both collapsed against the now warm metal of the machine behind her.

****

They dressed in the dark, silent in their thoughts. Logan found a bathroom and they took turns freshening up, and as she came out, he caught her hand. She met his gaze and then they both laughed.

"I can't believe we just did that." He'd turned on a light and he could see how flushed her face still was, but it was a good look. Yes, they'd been carried away by passion and probably shouldn't have, but there'd been none of the desperate edge to it that she'd had before. She really had let herself begin the healing process. So he didn't apologize.

She stole a shy look at him. "We didn't use a condom."

He raised an eyebrow. "No, I guess we didn't." To be honest, it hadn't even occurred to him.

"You don't have to worry. I had myself tested for—well, everything—when I got home. It was all negative, thank God." A look of sadness crossed her face. "And I'm on birth control."

"I cannot begin to tell you how happy it makes me to hear you say that." He kissed her lightly. "Because it means you are accepting that you are an amazing woman worth taking care of." He paused, almost dreading her answer to his next question. "How long are you going to stay?"

"Two weeks." She answered him so quickly, he knew she'd been anticipating him asking.

"And then what?" He took both her hands. "I don't want just this for a little while, Rachel. I want you. All the time."

"But you don't know me." She squeezed his hands and looked at him intently. "Not really. You know—that." She gestured at the dryer with a little smile. "God yes, you know that me. And you know the shy little girl I used to be when I knew Nora, and you know the messed up me, but you don't know me. Hell, I don't even know me. I've been so screwed up, it's been like being sick. And what it's left of me, the woman that stayed. Well, I've still got to get to know her."

"I'd like to help you do that."

"And I'd like that too." She smiled at him. "And you can, but only partway. I have to do the rest myself. So I'll stay for two weeks. And we'll see what happens. And then I'll go home for a while and work and find a place to stay and maybe you can visit me there when you can. And who knows?" She laughed. "My schedule's open now. I can see clearly for the first time in years, but I just don't know what I'm looking at yet."

He nodded, smiled, kissed her hands. "I understand. But I think I have an idea what you're looking at."

"I forgot." She smiled. "You're magic."

"Yes, and though fortune telling has never been my thing, I believe I can see into your future." He put his arm around her and led her to the door, flinging it open. "First, you're looking at a visit with my daughter and my friends. And later, when we're alone, definitely more of that, just not on a dryer this time."

"In a bed sounds good." She leaned her head against his shoulder. "Tell me more."

"Well, over the next two weeks, you're going to have so much fun snorkeling and dancing and playing with Jasmine—and me—that when it comes time to put you back on that plane, you're not going to want to leave. And beyond that?" He shrugged. "I see a lot of me convincing you to come back here. And you'll stay longer and longer each time until finally you just stay. And we live happily ever after."

"Hmm." She hugged his arm as they walked back toward the bar where his friends and family waited. "You may be right, and it certainly sounds good. And if it's true, you'd make a hell of a psychic."

"I'm not a psychic." He paused in the shadows just before they stepped into the ring of light and activity around the pool bar. He snapped his fingers, producing a small shower of sparks, and laughed at the wonder in her eyes. "I'm a magician." And then he took her hand and pulled her, unresisting, into his family circle.

About the Author

Michelle Garren Flye is an award-winning romance author. Reviewers have described her work as: "an engaging novel with charming and likable characters", a story that "will make you believe in love and second chances", and a "well-written and thought-provoking novel."

Michelle placed third in the Hyperink Romance Writing Contest for her short story "Life After". Her short stories have been published by the romance anthology Foreign Affairs, Opium.com, SmokelongQuarterly.com and Flashquake.com. She has served on the editorial staffs of Horror Library Butcher Shop Quartet and Tattered Souls.

Michelle has a Bachelor's degree in Journalism and Mass Communication from the University of North Carolina at Chapel Hill and a Master's degree in Library and Information Science from the University of North Carolina at Greensboro. She is the mother of three and lives in North Carolina with her husband and their rapidly growing collection of pets.

Also by Michelle Garren Flye:

Sleight of Hand Series:
Close Up Magic

Escape Magic

Island Magic

Carolina Wine Country:
Ducks in a Row

Saturday Love

Agapi Mou (Coming in 2015)

Published by Carina Press:
Where the Heart Lies

Published by Lyrical Press:
Secrets of the Lotus

Winter Solstice

Set in the North Carolina Mountains:

Weeds and Flowers

Tracks in the Sand

Did you enjoy this book? Consider leaving a review on Amazon, Barnes & Noble and GoodReads! I love hearing from my readers.

Here's what reviewers have said about some of my other work:

"Michelle Garren Flye is a wizard with words and I completely enjoyed her voice." --LAS Reviews

"...a well written sweet story that renews our faith in happily ever after." --Michelle Bowman, We Love Kink

"I highly recommend this unsettling book."
--Lauren Strait, Amazon Reviewer

"...well-written and thought-provoking novel..."
--Book Reviews & More by Kathy

"...a poignant story of loss, grief, secrets, love, redemption and second chances." --Jersey Girl Book Reviews

"...a book that will take you on a trip where failing or giving up is NOT an option."--Bunny's Book Reviews

"This book has so much depth on so many levels. The thought process, and how everything played out was so great!" --We're Jumpin' Books

"Readers will feel good and happy about this story... it made me smile." --Guilty Indulgence Romance Review

"Michelle has a way with words, she draws you into the small town life of these characters and keeps you hooked until the last page." — Stitch Read Cook

"...a well-written romantic novel with an unusual amount of depth." –Book Addiction